CARVE THE HEART

The Jack Palace Series

Yard Dog
Carve the Heart

A.G. PASQUELLA

THE JACK PALACE SERIES

CARVE THE HEART

DUNDURN
TORONTO

Publisher: Scott Fraser | Editor: Allison Hirst
Cover designer: Laura Boyle | Cover image: shutterstock.com/LesleyRigg
Printer: Webcom, a division of Marquis Book Printing Inc.

Library and Archives Canada Cataloguing in Publication

Title: Carve the heart / A.G. Pasquella.
Names: Pasquella, A. G., author.
Description: Series statement: Jack Palace series ; 2
Identifiers: Canadiana (print) 20190086416 | Canadiana (ebook) 20190086475 | ISBN 9781459742499
  (softcover) | ISBN 9781459742505 (PDF) | ISBN 9781459742512 (EPUB)
Classification: LCC PS8631.A8255 C37 2019 | DDC C813/.6—dc23

 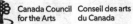

We acknowledge the support of the Canada Council for the Arts and the Ontario Arts Council for our publishing program. We also acknowledge the financial support of the Government of Ontario, through the Ontario Book Publishing Tax Credit and Ontario Creates, and the Government of Canada.

VISIT US AT

 dundurn.com | @dundurnpress |  dundurnpress | dundurnpress

Dundurn
3 Church Street, Suite 500
Toronto, Ontario, Canada
M5E 1M2

For Emma

CHAPTER 1

Real crime isn't like it is in the movies. It's not that glamorous. No one's zipping around the Italian countryside in a little sports car loaded with gold. Real crime is stupid, ugly, and violent.

The man in the alley had a woman pinned against a jet-black Cadillac Escalade. There was another man in the driver's seat. Both of the men had slicked-back dark hair that was shaved on the sides. The man pinning the woman was wearing a dark-blue track suit with white piping along the legs. He had a shitty goatee sprouting from his chin like moss. The woman was taller than the man. She was wearing a black leather skirt and a white jacket. Her brown hair was pulled back in a sleek, long ponytail. Her eyes were red like she'd been crying. The man was muttering something and she was shaking her head "no." I saw the man's face curdle. He raised his hand to slap her.

"Let her go."

Startled, the man turned toward me. Then he turned back to the woman. "Denise, I'm sorry. Baby, come on. I'm sorry."

Denise shook off the man and stepped away from the car. Her heels click-clacked on the concrete. She muttered, "Call the police," as she walked away.

I kept my eyes on the man. I could see his buddy peering at me in the driver's side mirror. The man with the mossy goatee tilted his chin at me. "You gonna call the cops?"

I nodded. "That's what she asked me to do, so I'll do it. But not just yet."

The man smirked. I hit him so hard his head snapped back and cracked against the car window.

The guy in the driver's seat fumbled with the door. I let him open it, then slammed it on him, hard. He yowled. I threw the door open and yanked the guy out. He blinked when he saw his buddy stretched out on the concrete. I hit him in the stomach and he doubled over, gasping.

"You watch for the cops while your buddy beats up women, is that it?"

The driver groaned, still doubled up. I could see a bald patch under his gel-slick hair. These guys were both wearing enough aftershave to start a small fire.

"Give me your wallet."

"Come on, man."

"Wallet."

Coughing, the driver slapped his wallet into my hand. There was probably about three hundred bucks in crisp green twenties inside. I ignored the money and pulled out his driver's licence. I made sure he saw me staring at his name, then I stuffed the licence back in the wallet and dropped it at his feet. "Well, Dimitri, now I know where you live. If you and Captain Asshole here" — I gave the man on the ground a nudge with the steel toe of my boot, making him grunt — "if you guys ever bother anyone else, I'll come looking for you." I reached into my jacket and pulled out a knife. I held it to Dimitri's throat, the blade glittering in the light. "Understand?"

"Y-yes."

I pointed to the man on the ground. "Go on, get your garbage and get the fuck out of here."

I tucked the knife back into its sheath beneath my jacket and strode down the alley. I stood watching as the driver stuffed the short man with the mossy goatee into the back seat of the Escalade. Then the driver pulled himself back into the driver's seat and the vehicle peeled out of the alley. *All aboard the Douche Express, last stop: who the fuck cares?*

A rusty door opened into the alley. My buddy Eddie Yao stood there in his charcoal-grey pinstripe suit, a chrome .45 in his hand. "All good?"

I shook my head. "Assholes like that don't learn. Do me a favour, will ya? Give the cops a call."

Eddie blinked. "What?"

"She asked me to call." I shrugged. "You still have a guy at the precinct, right?"

Eddie nodded. "I'll take care of it." His eyes scanned the alley and then he beckoned me closer. "Come on down."

"Another time. I got Melody upstairs." Melody and I had been drinking and getting frisky when the Escalade bros started roughing up the woman. You never treat a woman like that, especially not in the alley behind my office.

Eddie tucked his .45 back into the shoulder holster beneath his suit jacket. He didn't smile, but his eyes twinkled. "Trust me, Jack. You're going to want to see this."

I stepped through the doorway, and the heavy steel door slammed closed.

I followed Eddie down a set of dingy stairs. It looked like the beginning of every horror movie ever. All it needed was a few bloody handprints on the wall. At the bottom was another door. Standing in front of the door was Eddie's guy Josh, wearing a black suit that seemed to blend into the shadows. Josh nodded his head and opened the door.

Once we passed through, the whole horror-show vibe disappeared. This was Eddie's basement casino, and it was classy, man, classy. Deep-maroon walls and polished oak chairs. Croupiers and dealers in maroon vests and black bowties. The gamblers were a different story. Eddie's place attracted them all: the whales, the sharks, the donkeys, and the grinders. Everyone was trying to turn cards into money. An acne-scarred man with mirrored sunglasses and a straw cowboy hat tapped the felt at one of the blackjack tables, calling for one more card. As Eddie and I walked past the tables, no one looked up.

Eddie opened the door to his office and grinned. "After you."

"I hate it when you're all mysterious and shit."

Eddie's eyes twinkled again. He gestured toward the open door.

I stepped inside and froze. There was a beautiful woman sitting behind Eddie's desk. She had pale skin, dark eyes, and jet-black hair. She was wearing a black turtleneck and a light-grey blazer. Her silver earrings caught the light as she turned toward the door. We made eye contact. She didn't smile.

"Jack."

"Cassandra."

I hadn't seen her in years — ten, to be exact. We dated, I loved her, she left me. It wasn't quite that simple, but that was the gist of it.

Eddie gave the red leather chair in front of his desk a tug and a pat. "Have a seat, Jack. Can I get you guys anything? Cassie, another Scotch?"

She nodded. I sat down in the chair. The cushion deflated under my weight. "I'll have a Scotch, too." I stared at Eddie, trying to beam thoughts into his brain. *Goddamn, Eddie. Warn a fella, would ya?*

Eddie just smiled and walked out the door.

Cassandra stared at me from across Eddie's desk. I stared back. The clock on the wall tick-tocked. Finally, she sighed. "I'll get right to it. Jack, I need your help."

CHAPTER 2

Eddie came back with the Scotch. Cassandra reached for her glass. I blinked. Her right hand was mottled and twisted with old burns. It looked like a discarded snakeskin. "What happened to your hand?"

"Tactful as always, Jack." She sipped her Scotch.

I gulped mine and the Scotch burned down my throat. I felt the familiar warmth spread through my belly. Melody was upstairs waiting for me. I pictured her naked body, her blond hair fanned out on my blue velour couch. "Let's make this quick. I've got someone waiting for me upstairs."

Cassandra smiled. "You're a popular guy."

"That's me, Mr. Popular."

Cassandra glanced over at Eddie. He looked down at his clunky gold Rolex. "Oh, look at the time. I've got to, uh …" Eddie trailed off. As he headed back to the door, he looked over his shoulder and gave me a wink. "Let me know if you guys need anything else."

Eddie closed the door behind him. Cassandra reached into her little black leather purse, pulled out a tissue, and dabbed at her eyes. At first I thought it was just theatre, but when she looked over at me, her eyes were glistening. "I won't lie, Jack. Things have gone a little bit sideways."

"That happens." I sipped my Scotch. "Why come to me?"

Cassandra stared at me with her dark eyes. "You know I wouldn't be here if I didn't have to. I'm here because I have no other choice."

"I'll find you someone else. I know a lot of guys who could help. Ritchie Quan's set up shop just down the street."

Cassandra screwed up her face like she just sucked a lemon. "That pervert who always smells like soup?"

"All right, not Ritchie then. Remember Camille? She's working for Iron Sphinx. Big security firm, totally legit."

Cassandra shook her head. "I need someone I can trust. Someone discreet." She stared into my eyes. "I need you."

I thought about Melody, waiting for me upstairs. She was probably wondering where the hell I was. Either that or she had fallen asleep.

"I'll help you. But I need some more information."

"All right." Cassandra closed her eyes and took a deep breath. "I'll just lay it all out here. I had a backer. His name is Anton. I don't want to work with him anymore." Cassandra bit her nails. "But he doesn't want to let me go."

"He wants to continue the partnership."

"Yeah." Cassandra's eyes were watery, but she smiled. God, she had a beautiful smile. "That's it in a nutshell. Last week, Anton fronted me the buy-in for a private game. A hundred large." She grinned. "You should've seen it, Jack. At one point I was up like three hundred grand. I caught a queen of spades on the river to make a beautiful flush. But then the cards dried up." She shook her head. "Pretty sure the game was rigged."

"Who was running it?"

"Does it matter?"

I just stared at her.

She sighed. "It was Freddy Johns. I know, I know. I should've known better. Freddy's a snake, but his games are big money. I needed a win, Jack. I've had a really bad run. I'm up against the wall here."

"How much do you owe Anton?"

Cassandra fiddled with the strap of her black leather purse, then went back to biting her nails.

I made my voice gentle. "How much, Cassie?"

"Six."

"Six …"

"Six large." She looked up at me, her eyes flashing. "I owe him six hundred thousand dollars, all right?"

"Jesus."

"I don't need a lecture." She rubbed her temples. "I know things have gotten out of hand. Anton's pushing me into some dangerous games, asking me to do things I don't want to do. I told him he'll get his money, but we should break off the partnership and go our separate ways. He didn't think that was such a good idea."

"Did he —"

"He never hit me, if that's what you're asking."

"Your hand —"

"Jesus, Jack, give it a rest." Cassandra hid her burned right hand under Eddie's desk. "Yes, Anton's violent. I've seen him do some horrible, horrible shit. At first, though, he was good to me." Cassandra smiled a crooked half smile. "Go on, call me an idiot."

"You're not an idiot." I paused. "He threatened you?"

"Yes." Her eyes welled up again. "He said if I ever tried to leave, he would kill me."

I wanted to jump up and go find Anton right then and there. I wanted to grab the man by the hair and smash his face into a wall until his face was gone.

Instead, I forced myself to be calm. Breathe in, breathe out. "Anton. He's connected?"

"Oh yeah. He's part of this big eastern European crew. Heroin, mostly. Some synthetics."

"How'd you meet this guy?"

"We never fucked, if that's what you're asking."

I held out my hands. "Hey, I didn't ask."

"And now you don't have to." She smiled that sad little half smile. "Where do you think we met, Jack? We met at a poker game. He liked the way I played."

"Simple as that, huh?"

"Simple as that."

"All right." I ran my hand through my hair. These days it was more silver than brown. "Eddie's got a safe house in Scarborough. You can stay there tonight." I stood up.

"And tomorrow?"

"I'll talk to Anton. Get him to back off."

Cassandra collapsed back into Eddie's chair. I could see the relief on her face. "Thanks, Jack."

CHAPTER 3

I left Cassandra with Eddie and headed up the stairs. Eddie's restaurant was on the first floor. At this time of night I could hear drunken students laughing loudly, clattering their forks while they scarfed down their chicken balls with red sauce. I kept going up the dusty wooden stairs to the second floor. At the end of the hallway was the door to my office. It looked like a wooden door, but it was actually a thin wood veneer glued on top of steel. If anyone ever tried to kick down my door, their leg would shatter like glass.

I fumbled with my keys and unlocked the locks. I had four of them on the door, plus two security cameras, one hidden discretely near the door and another facing the stairs. I liked to think I was cautious, not paranoid. I swung open the door and stepped inside.

Most of the lights were off. My desk lamp was glowing a warm orange. The plant on my desk bobbed slightly. It looked like it was waving. I nodded to the plant. "Hello, plant." There was an almost-empty bourbon bottle and two empty glasses over by the couch. I didn't see Melody anywhere. Then the door to the bathroom opened and Melody stepped out, fully dressed. She was wearing skin-tight black leggings and a white T-shirt that had a black-and-white picture of a unicorn on it. Her blond hair was pulled back in a messy high ponytail. She saw me and laughed. I loved her laugh. It sounded like a cascade of silver bells. "Well, don't look so happy to see me."

I gestured to her outfit. "You put on clothes."

"Yep." She grinned. "I've got to go to work."

"I thought you had the night off."

She stepped closer and gave me a hug. She smelled like summertime, like coconut oil and the beach. "There you go again, thinking too much. That's going to get you in trouble." She smiled up at me. One of her upper teeth was adorably crooked. "Ride to the club with me."

"Can't do it, babe. Eddie and I have to drop off a client."

"A client? Ooh la la. Look at you, gettin' paid."

She strutted over to the couch and grabbed her white leather purse. The fringe on the purse swayed as she slung it over her shoulder. "All right, I'll see you at the club later. I've gotta stop by my place first. Pick up my work outfit. I wasn't supposed to work tonight but someone called in sick." She shrugged. "What the heck, right? Money is money."

We kissed. Her lips tasted like raspberries. I watched her sashay out the door. Then I walked over to the nearly empty bourbon bottle. For a second I thought about just guzzling it straight from the bottle, but I'm not an animal. I splashed the last of the bourbon into one of the heavy glass tumblers and chugged it. Then I went down the stairs to meet Cassandra and Eddie.

Eddie's guy Josh had already pulled the car around. The coal-black Lexus was waiting for us in the alley behind Eddie's building. It was the end of June, which in theory was the start of summertime, but the cold night air was still slicing right through my jacket. Josh slapped the keys into Eddie's hand, and then Eddie, Cassandra, and I bundled into the car. The inside of Eddie's Lexus was impeccably clean. The interior smelled like spearmint gum. We all buckled up and Eddie revved the engine. We rumbled through the alley, past the graffiti and the garbage cans. Then we headed south on side streets over to Sullivan. We cut across the northbound lanes of Spadina and headed south again, past the late-night crowds and neon signs and stacks of garbage, down to the Gardiner.

The expressway took us east. Eddie grinned. "Did I ever tell you about my time as a street racer?"

"Yeah. Plenty."

Cassandra leaned forward. "You never told me."

Eddie looked up at the rear-view and winked at Cassie. "I was fast, man. In another life, I could've been a pro. Back when I was younger, my friends and I would blast souped-up Honda Civics across empty highways at three in the morning. Then one night, this guy I was racing took a turn too fast." Eddie shook his head sadly. He reached into his jacket pocket and pulled out a cigarette. "That guy died. Me, I wanted to stay alive."

Cassandra tilted her chin toward the cigarette in Eddie's hand. "Then you should throw those things in the garbage."

Eddie grunted. "That's what my daughter says, too."

"She's right."

Eddie tossed the cigarette out the window and gunned the engine. The expressway rose up on big concrete pillars. Down below and to the right was the lake. The moonlight glinted off the water.

I peeked back at Cassandra. She was sitting straight up, looking prim and proper in her black turtleneck and grey blazer, as if she were on her way to a job interview. She saw me looking at her and gave me a nod. The nod was strangely formal. I nodded back and then looked straight ahead at traffic.

She had walked out on me ten years ago. I hadn't seen her since, until tonight. What had happened in those ten years? I didn't know much. She played cards, she met Anton, her hand got burned. Maybe that was all I needed to know. That and the fact that she owed Anton six large. Still, I couldn't help being curious. A lot could happen in ten years.

We headed north on the DVP. We drove in silence until Eddie reached down and turned on the radio. Mellow jazz filled the car. We sailed on, past the Aga Khan Museum. I had never been, but I heard it was nice. Tapestries and mosaics, stuff like that.

We left the DVP and went east on the 401. Fifteen minutes later, we left the highway and hit the side streets. Ten minutes after that, we were at the safe house.

We stepped out of the car and into the cool night air. Maybe it was my imagination, but the air smelled fresher here. More grass, less concrete. The safe house driveway shone black beneath the street lights. It had recently been redone. Eddie knew a driveway guy.

Eddie, Cassandra, and I walked up to the porch and Eddie knocked on the door. Cousin Vin opened the door. Vin shifted, revealing the gun in his left hand, which he had been holding behind the door. He tucked the pistol into his pants. "Hiya, Jack. How's tricks?"

"Silly Vin. Tricks are for kids."

Vin frowned. "That's the rabbit cereal, right? I mean with the cartoon rabbit, not, like, actually made from rabbits."

"Two scoops of rabbits in Kellogg's Rabbit Bran." I stepped past Vin into the living room.

Eddie had bought this place for a song back in the Toronto housing bust of the early 1990s. His Aunt Cecilia's name was on the lease. She was never here, though, and that was a good thing. She was a tough old broad who had raised six kids. All six of them had grown up to be gangsters. Aunt Cecilia herself sat at the top of a numbers-running racket. I saw her sometimes at Eddie's get-togethers. She kept to herself in a quiet corner of the yard, just her and her phone and her pad of paper. Making calls, taking bets.

Cassandra stood in the living room of the safe house and glanced around. I watched her as she took it all in. "Well, this is cute."

I had no idea who decorated the house. Maybe it was Eddie himself. I'd have to ask him sometime. Whoever it was had really done a bang-up job. It looked exactly like a little old lady actually lived there. All the lamps and the tables and the chairs were at least thirty years old. The TV looked prehistoric, like an appliance from *The Flintstones*. There were vases stuffed with dried flowers as far as the eye could see. Framed family photos were scattered about on the end tables and the walls. I didn't recognize any of the people. For all I knew, the pictures had come with the frames. There were a few dolls and stuffed animals on the pale-pink couch. The place even smelled old.

I pointed down the hall. "Bedroom's that way. There's another TV and some DVDs. You ever see *The River Wild*? I think that's in there."

Cassandra smiled. "I always think Laura Dern is in that movie. But she isn't."

"Meryl Streep," Vin chimed in. We all turned toward him. Vin suddenly looked sheepish. "She's good in it, too," he muttered.

Cassandra and I walked down the hallway to the bedroom. The bedroom was small and sparse: a double bed topped with an orange comforter, a dresser with a television on top, a nightstand with a clock radio and another vase stuffed with dried flowers. Cassandra picked up a stack of DVDs from the dresser and flipped through them. "You guys need to modernize. Everything's on Netflix now."

"Hopefully you won't be here long enough for binge watching."

Cassandra sat down on the edge of the bed. She looked up at me with her dark eyes. "Go on, say it."

"Say what?"

"Say I'm an idiot. Say I never should've gone into business with Anton."

I shook my head. "That doesn't matter now. The important thing is what comes next."

Cassie looked down at her burned hand. "I should've walked away from Anton a long time ago. But I just couldn't do it."

"Why not? You did it to me."

Cassandra flinched. Instantly I wished I could press a button and rewind time. "Shit. Sorry."

Cassandra straightened up. "No. I'm glad you brought it up. We had to talk about it sooner or later. I'm not ashamed of what I did. Leaving you took a lot of courage. You're a violent man, Jack. A lot of women get killed trying to leave violent men."

I blinked. "You thought I was going to kill you?"

"I didn't know. That was the scary part."

"I would never have hurt you."

"I know." Cassandra looked away. "But then again, that's what they all say."

CHAPTER 4

I woke up hungover, but that was nothing new. I peeled myself off the couch, stumbled over to my tiny office bathroom, and splashed some cold water on my face. I filled up my chipped white mug and drank deep. Bit by bit, I was starting to feel halfway human.

Sunlight was pouring through my office windows. The red digital numbers on my clock radio said 10:20 a.m. I walked over to my desk and pulled a cheap burner phone out of the top drawer. I punched in Cassandra's number. "How'd you sleep?" I asked.

"Like a baby — by which I mean I woke up crying every fifteen minutes." Cassandra laughed. "I'm just kidding. I slept fine. You?"

I glanced over at the blue couch where I had passed out last night. "Just fine. I'll come pick you up, okay? Let's grab some brunch." Back when we were dating, we'd never had brunch. Two a.m. diner eats were more our thing. Brunch was for people who woke up in the morning. "I need you to tell me where Anton hangs out."

"He's usually —"

"Not on the phone. Tell me when I see you."

We said our goodbyes, then I called Melody. The phone rang five times before she picked up. "Hello?"

I could hear the sleep in her voice. "Sorry to wake you."

"Aw, Jack, what the fuck, man? What time is it?"

"It's almost ten-thirty."

"You never made it to the club last night."

"Something came up with my client."

"Yeah, yeah. I'm going in for the lunchtime rush today. Give me a lift?"

"Yeah, okay."

I heard Melody inhale and then exhale — her first cigarette of the morning. "My hero. You just saved me cab fare." I could practically hear her grinning over the phone.

I said goodbye, hung up, and slid the burner back into the desk drawer. The timing would be tight, but if I hustled I could do it. I reached for my jacket and headed out the door.

Eddie let me borrow a car. Not the Lexus. Only he drove that. Cassandra came bursting out of the safe house as soon as I pulled into the drive. Vin poked his head around the door and scanned the street. He saw me and nodded. I nodded back and Vin's head disappeared.

Cassandra slid into the passenger seat and held out her burned hand. "Jack."

I shook her hand gingerly. Another strangely formal greeting. "Cassandra."

"You don't have to worry." She held her hand up. "It doesn't hurt. Not anymore."

"You ever gonna tell me what happened?"

"Probably." Cassandra smiled. "One of these days." She looked down at her outfit. The same black turtleneck, grey blazer, and black pants from yesterday. "I need to go shopping at some point and get some clean clothes."

"I could run back to your place and pick something up."

Cassandra shook her head. "Anton was putting me up in a hotel. Nothing fancy, but it was a roof over my head. I can't go back there, though." Cassandra plucked her sleeve. "These will be all right for one more day."

I looked down at my jacket and black pants. I was wearing my yesterday clothes, too.

Cassandra gave my outfit the once-over. "You can pull off that rumpled look. Me, not so much."

"You look …" *Adorable*, I'd been about to say. I choked off the word before it left my mouth. "Fine. You look fine."

"I'm starving."

"Then let's go eat."

There was a little family-run diner a few blocks from the safe house. They had breakfast, fresh fruit, all that good shit.

Our server poured coffee. She was beautiful. She was young and healthy and she glowed. I felt like a troll that had just crawled out from under a bridge. We ordered our food and the server sashayed away. I sipped slowly, feeling that hot rush of caffeine. Ah, caffeine. The most socially acceptable drug there is.

We sat in silence for a while. All around us, people talked and laughed. Silverware clattered. People typed on laptops and stared at their phones. Our server brought the food. Cassandra pushed bits of blueberry pancake around on her plate. I had a bowl of oatmeal because I was serious about my health and a side of bacon because I wasn't that serious. I wiped oatmeal off my face with a scratchy paper napkin. Cassandra glanced toward the window, then back at me.

"So. Anton."

I waited. Cassie exhaled, long and low. "He lives downtown, I think. One night he took me to a penthouse down at Queen's Quay. He didn't say, but I got the impression it was his." Cassandra looked down at her plate and then back at me. "He's out of the country a lot. He might be a hard guy to find."

I took a sip of coffee. "I'll find him." I leaned forward, my eyes locked on to Cassandra. "We'll have to work out a payment plan. He's not going to let you skate on the money."

Cassandra looked down. She twisted the paper napkin in her hands. "I know. I, uh … I was hoping to borrow some from you."

I blinked. "You think I've got six large?"

"Well. I was kind of hoping."

I just stared at her. She reached across the table and took my hand. "I know what you're thinking. Here comes this broad you haven't seen in a decade. And now she's asking you to help her out of a jam and, oh by the way, can she borrow six hundred thousand dollars?" Cassandra nodded to herself. "I know it doesn't look good. But what can I do? I'm out of options here, Jack."

I pulled my hand away. "I don't have that kind of money."

"Eddie …"

I set down my coffee cup. "Eddie's cash flow is tight. Even if he had the cash, he's not going to just let you walk off with six large."

Cassandra shook her head. "I'm not walking anywhere. I'm good for it, Jack." She pushed her plate away. "I'd rather owe the money to Eddie than to Anton."

"Eddie's got silent partners. They don't lend money." My eyes flickered down to her burned hand. I looked away. "Anton isn't going to let you go easily."

"I know. That's why I'm here."

"What exactly do you want me to do, Cassie? Threaten him? Punch him in the face? Dangle his ass off a rooftop?"

She smiled. "Just his ass?"

"You know what I mean."

"I don't know, Jack. I just — I don't know, okay? Talk to him. Make him go away." She rubbed her eyes. "I'm so tired."

I reached over the table and gave her arm an awkward pat. "We're going to work it out." My eyes flickered to the clock on the wall. "Shit. I gotta go."

"Can I come, too?" Cassandra grimaced. "The safe house is nice and all, but after awhile it feels like the walls are closing in."

"I get that." I thought back to my time in prison. Those nights when the cell walls started to crush me like the trash compactor in *Star Wars*. "I'm picking up the woman I'm seeing. Gonna give her a ride to work."

Cassandra's eyebrows shot up. "Oh. If you think I should —"

"No, no —"

"Because I could stay ..."

"It's okay." I grinned. "Who knows, maybe you guys will hit it off."

We climbed back into Eddie's car and buckled up. I stomped on the accelerator and we sailed down toward Queen and Pape. It was going to take about thirty minutes. If we hit the lights just right, I'd be on time to pick up Melody.

I glanced over at Cassandra. "So. What've you been up to for the past ten years?"

She smiled her sad crooked half smile. "Just sum up a decade, huh? I bet I can do it in three words. 'This and that.'"

"C'mon. You can do better than that."

"I've been playing poker, Jack. After I left you and moved out of my place, I hit the road and headed south. I stayed away from Vegas because Vegas was too obvious. I went to Mississippi and hit the riverboat circuit." She shook her head. "It's not glamorous. The days of petticoats and handlebar moustaches are long gone. But there's poker games in them thar riverboats, and you know a gal's gotta earn a living."

"When did you meet Anton?"

Cassie was quiet for a while. "It seems like a million years ago. Other times, it seems like it was just yesterday."

"But —"

"About three years ago." Cassandra raised her burned hand to her mouth and bit her nails. "I was in a tough spot and he helped me out."

Cassandra fell silent. I knew enough not to push further. Instead, I turned on the radio. Funky New Orleans jazz filled the car. Trombone Shorty's cover of "Here Come the Girls."

We rumbled across Queen Street East and then turned south on Pape. We passed tumbledown duplexes with crooked concrete stairs and weeds poking through the cracks. There was a public housing unit on the other side of the street. Farther south at Pape and Eastern was a movie studio where no doubt some quality entertainment was being churned out right this minute. I screeched the car to a halt.

Cassandra glanced out the window. "This is Melody's place?"

"Yep." I pointed to a tidy semi-detached house on the west side of the street. "That's her house right there."

"You and Melody. How long's that been going on?"

"Not long. Three months. I was doing some security at the club where she works." Silence hung heavy in the car. "So, uh … you dating anyone?"

Cassandra shook her head. "Nope. Not right now."

I peered out the car windows. I didn't see any signs of trouble. Farther up the street, a kid was riding his bike in slow, lazy circles. A man and a woman were walking south. The woman was carrying a bag from the liquor store. The man held some records under his arm. I had a feeling their day was going to be a lot better than mine.

The door to Melody's duplex banged open and a scraggly man in a stained white undershirt and droopy cargo shorts came storming out. The man was clutching a cardboard box in his hands. He thudded down the porch steps, walked to the sidewalk, and slammed down his box. He reached into it and pulled out an old-fashioned answering machine and a hammer. He then proceeded to beat the shit out of the answering machine. Bits of the machine flew up into the air.

Cassandra frowned. "What the hell?"

I was wondering the same thing. The door opened again and Melody stepped out onto the porch. She was wearing big clunky sunglasses with white frames, tight black yoga pants, and a T-shirt with a silk-screened picture of a cat on it. She stood watching the man smash up the answering machine for a minute, then she leaned against the porch railing and lit up a cigarette.

Box Man kicked broken answering machine bits into the road, then picked up his box and walked across the street. He pulled a screwdriver out of the box and dropped it down a sewer grate. Then he pulled out a pair of pliers and dropped them down into the sewer as well. Then he put what looked like a bright-orange tape measure onto the sewer grate and started bashing it to bits with the hammer.

Cassandra and I kept watching. She turned to me. "Is he destroying evidence?"

I shook my head. "He's drunk or high or something. Who knows what he's doing."

Box Man, still with the hammer in his hand, straightened up and started stalking back across the street toward Melody.

"Shit." I reached for the door handle. "Stay in the car, Cassie."

The bright June sun hit me right in the eyes as I stepped into the street. Melody was standing on the porch with her hands on her hips, a burning cigarette drooping from her lip like she was a Wild West gun-fighter. She watched Box Man storm closer with the hammer in his hand.

Box Man turned and saw me coming. His eyes were bloodshot and wide with rage. He snarled and swung. He was drunk and slow. I sidestepped and the hammer went wide.

The trick to punching is you don't aim for the guy's face. You aim for the back of his head. I swung, picturing my fist plowing right through the man's skull. Box Man went down, out cold. I gave my hand a shake.

Melody peeled herself off the porch railing and flicked her lit cigarette at the unconscious man. "That's what you get. Jack, you want some ice?"

My hand throbbed. "Nah, I'll be okay." I gestured to the man sprawled out on the sidewalk. "What the hell was that about?"

"Aah." Melody waved her hand, dismissing the man on the ground. "That's Gord. He's just a contractor I know. He came by drunk out of his head trying to sell me this box of rusty crap." Melody looked down at the unconscious man. "I don't know why he thought I'd want a box full of old broke-ass tools."

I looked down at the man, taking in his dirty clothes, his dust-coloured skin. "He's an addict."

"Yeah, probably."

"He needed a fix, so he needed money. Thought maybe you'd be a soft touch. It's a variation of the construction scam. Guy drives around residential neighbourhoods until he sees a house being built. He makes sure the crew is all gone for the day. Then he knocks on a neighbour's door and says something like, 'Hi, my name's Bobby, I was doing some work next door but they forgot to pay me. Could you loan me twenty dollars and they'll pay it back to you tomorrow?' It's a desperate ploy, but sometimes it works. Then the addict takes that twenty and it's off to the crack house."

I glanced over my shoulder. People were standing at their windows, peering through the curtains. I heard sirens in the distance. "Come on. It's time to get gone."

We left Gord the contractor lying on the sidewalk and hustled over to the car. Well, I hustled. Melody sashayed. She was carrying her white leather-fringe purse and a red gym bag. I half-expected her to pull a lollipop out of her pocket and start sucking on it.

When we got to the car, I opened the back door for her. Her carefully tweezed and plucked eyebrows shot up behind her sunglasses. "Back seat, Jack? Really?" Without waiting for an answer, she slid inside.

I got into the driver's seat, fired up the engine, and floored it. Best not to be here when the cops arrived. Some diligent citizen might've copied down the digits of the licence plate, but that could be fixed. I'm sure Eddie had some spare plates lying around somewhere.

Melody leaned forward, peering over the top of her sunglasses. Her gold bracelets jangled as she held out a hand. "Hi, I'm Melody."

Cassandra reached back with her left hand. "Cassandra."

"So, Jack's helping you out, huh? Oh, don't worry, he didn't tell me shit. He keeps all that client stuff really close to his vest. Confidentiality and all that." She reached out and gave my shoulder a pat. "He's a good guy, this guy. You can trust him."

Cassandra turned and shot me her crooked smile. "Good to know."

Melody glanced back and forth from Cassandra to me. "So … you guys want to talk business or what? I've got my Walkman right here." Melody rummaged through the red gym bag. "I put in these earbuds, man, I can't hear shit." Melody held up her Walkman. "Remember these? A bit before my time, but what the hell, I love the whole retro cassette thing. I buy 'em by the bagful from Value Village. I've picked up some real freaky shit, man."

Cassandra shot me another look. "I bet you're not the only one."

I frowned at Cassandra. *Cool it.*

"There's whole communities out there. You ever go on Reddit?"

"I'm not much of a cassette person."

"Oh, it's not just cassettes. They've got subreddits for whatever you're into. Do you like weed?"

"So, uh, Melody," I said, trying to reroute the conversation. "What's in the bag?"

She patted the red gym bag on the seat next to her. "My costume for tonight. At first I was going to do Sexy Cop, but then I thought, nah, fuck that, I'm goin' with Angel, baby. I broke out the wings and everything."

Cassandra glanced back at Melody. "You're a performer?"

"A dancer, yeah. Jack didn't tell you? I dance at the Starlight." Melody raised her arms toward the roof of Eddie's Camry and did a little shimmy. "I'm damn good, too."

"And Jack's your bodyguard?"

I shook my head. "I did some security work for the club."

"Yeah, until your ass got fired." Melody clapped her hands over her mouth. "Oh shit," she said, muffled. She moved her hands away. "I shouldn't have said that. Seriously, lady, don't worry, he's damn good at what he does."

Cassandra smiled. "Of that, I have no doubt."

The car engine thrummed. We carried on, heading west on Queen Street East. Melody sat quietly for a minute. Then she leaned toward Cassandra. "So, uh … what do you do?"

"I play poker."

"Oh yeah? Like, professionally?"

"That's right."

"Big money?"

"It can be." Cassandra turned away and glanced out the window. "Things are a bit rough right now."

She looked back at Melody. "Jack's going to help me straighten it out."

Melody grinned. "Who says chivalry is dead?"

I shook my head. "It's not like that."

Melody straightened up, pursed her lips, and said in a deep voice, "Just business, ma'am."

I looked up at the rear-view mirror and shot Melody a frown. "Yeah, that's right."

"Hey, I can dig it." Melody laughed. Her teeth sparkled in the sun. I knew most of her teeth were caps. She'd told me that a few months back: after a lifetime of hating her teeth, she'd shelled out the bucks for a brand new mouth. "I'm just yankin' your chain."

"Speaking of business," I said, "let's get you to work." I stomped on the accelerator and we headed for the Starlight.

Toronto's strip clubs were shutting down. It wasn't because of some moral crusade, some gallant charge led by the self-appointed, so-called forces of decency. Nope. The clubs were closing because of the internet, and also because of the real estate boom. Most strip clubs in the city were family-owned enterprises that had been entertaining horny businessmen and bachelor parties for decades. The club where Melody worked had twelve private booths where basically anything could happen if the price was right. But now all that was in danger of going the way of the dodo. Most of the old-school rub & tug parlours of sleazy 1970s Yonge Street were long gone, and the strip clubs were next on the chopping block. Real estate values were shooting through the roof, and realtors were calling the club owners daily. Someday in the not-too-distant future all the skin palaces would be gone, sold to the highest bidder, torn down and bull-dozed to make way for even more rickety towers of shoddily built and overpriced condos.

Today, though, the Starlight was open for business. Teeth-rattling techno bass boomed from the speakers. Girls dressed in lingerie sauntered through the crowd looking to sell private one-on-one dances. The girls were barely out of their teens. Steam rose from the trays of mac and cheese and chicken fingers sitting next to the wilted Caesar salad on the buffet table.

Cassandra made her scrunched-up just-sucked-a-lemon face as we walked past the buffet. "People eat here?"

"All the time." Bruno the club manager stepped toward us. "Food's actually pretty damn decent. Right, Jack?"

"Yeah, sure." The food was nothing to write home about. Starch and carbs to keep the businessmen glued to their seats. It was the casino model. Keep 'em here and keep 'em spending.

Bruno shook my hand. He tried the power squeeze. I squeezed his hand back, harder. The man winced. He pulled his hand free and glanced over at Melody. "You're late."

"Traffic." She shrugged. "Whatcha gonna do?"

"Leave earlier."

I shot him a smile. "You're a wise man, Bruno." He wasn't. He did the scut work while his silent partners stacked the cash.

Bruno chewed his toothpick, smoothed out his thick black moustache, and leered at Cassandra. "And who is this lovely young lady? You lookin' for work, sweetheart?"

"No." Cassandra looked at Bruno like he was a hairball coughed up by a sick cat. She tugged on my arm. "Come on, Jack. Let's go."

I turned to Melody. "You good?"

She grinned, flashing me those perfect store-bought teeth. "Yeah, yeah, I'm good. You run along and have fun."

Without another word, Cassandra spun on her heel and headed back through the lunchtime crowd. I followed.

"I still don't see why we had to walk her in," she said.

"There's a lot of weirdos out there. I don't have to tell you that. Sometimes these creeps get fixated on a girl. They wait for her outside the club."

"In broad daylight?"

"What can I say? Bad shit can happen around the clock."

Cassandra froze. "Oh shit."

"What?" My muscles tensed. I tried to follow Cassandra's gaze.

"Shit, shit, shit."

"Help me out here, Cassie."

"That guy over there with the shaved head and the grey goatee and the girl on his lap."

"I see him."

"That's Fisher. He's one of Anton's enforcers." Cassandra yanked on my hand. "Come on, we've got to go."

Fisher spotted us. He stood up abruptly, causing the dancer on his lap to fall to the floor. She shouted. He ignored her and headed toward us.

I didn't take my eyes off him. "Go over to the bar," I said to Cassandra. "Don't go outside. Anton's crew might be waiting. Just sit tight."

Fisher swaggered up to me. He was about six foot five. Taller than me. He was wearing a black T-shirt and a black leather jacket. His pants were black, too. Up close, I realized he was older than me, likely in his midsixties, but he was in great shape. He was probably well practiced in sending men half his age to the hospital. He gave me a nod. "Jack, right? Mr. Jack Palace."

"Fisher." We didn't shake hands.

"Heard you worked here."

"Your information's out of date."

"Oh yeah?" Fisher grinned. One of his gold teeth caught the light. "Couldn't keep your hands off the girls, huh?"

I just stared at him. He coughed and rubbed his nose. "Heard you know a friend of ours. She hasn't been coming to work lately. Her boss is startin' to get worried."

It was almost impossible to make out what Fisher was saying. There was the booming techno music, sure, but the real problem was The Mumble. Slurring, muttering, mumbling, covering your mouth — these were the old habits of a career criminal. Lowering your voice and slurring your words makes it harder to be understood on wiretaps. Covering your mouth makes it impossible for anyone watching to read your lips. Problem is, it also makes it hard for anyone who's supposed to be listening to understand, too. How many gangland killings were just the result of straight-up misunderstandings?

I cupped my ear. I kept my eye on Fisher's hands. "Sorry, can't hear you."

Fisher frowned. "Come back tonight. Ten o'clock. The boss wants to meet you." Fisher looked over my shoulder at Cassandra cowering by the bar. He winked. I wanted to reach in and yank his eye right out of its socket. Instead I watched as he turned and strolled out the front door. Cassandra sagged, visibly relieved.

I walked over and caught the bartender's eye. "Scotch. Make it a double. One for her, too." I slid a big tip across the bar.

Cassandra cupped her glass with both hands and drank deep. Then she turned to me. "How did he know we'd be here?"

The Scotch wasn't top shelf, but it would do. "Someone tipped him off." I drained my drink and set the glass on the bar. "Someone told him I still come here. So he came here looking for me."

Cassie's shoulders slumped. "And he found us."

"Yep." I narrowed my eyes and stared at the exits. "Fisher's probably out there right now waiting for us. If he thinks he can, he'll try to snatch you up. Don't look like that. I'm not trying to scare you. I'm just saying we've got to be careful."

"So how do we get out of here?"

"Follow me."

I took Cassandra by the hand and together we pushed through the crowd toward the stage. A dancer I didn't recognize was up there doing her thing. She was topless, her breasts surprisingly small for a strip club. The crowd didn't care. Red-faced businessmen hooted and clapped for more. The dancer teased them, snapping the elastic on her lacy white G-string. Bass boomed from the speakers and thudded against my heart.

I steered Cassandra past the crowd at the foot of the stage. We headed into a dark, narrow hallway to the right of the stage. At the end of the hall was a red exit sign. Cassandra headed toward the exit, but I shook my head. "Not yet." Instead we ducked through a door into a small room. There was a stack of cardboard boxes along one wall. Directly ahead of us was another door. A big bouncer sitting on a white metal folding stool next to the other door saw us come in and half-rose to his feet. Our eyes locked. The bouncer's face softened and he sat back down. "Hiya, Jack. Been awhile."

"Tomasso." I stepped forward and held out my hand. The big bouncer shook it. "We got a bit of a situation here." I gave him the Cliff's Notes recap: Anton, Fisher, Cassandra.

Tomasso's big brow furrowed. "That's fucked up."

"It is. So we need to get upstairs."

The giant bouncer rose to his feet. I saw Cassandra's eyes widen as Tomasso just kept going up. It was like watching a sped-up film of a redwood tree going from seed to sapling to sixty feet tall. "Come with me."

Tomasso threw open the second door and we filed backstage. The music was muffled here, but still loud. *You're getting old, Jack.* One of the dancers, Valerie, was adjusting her sequined bra. Her costume was covered with feathers. She ignored us, focused on the stage, waiting for her cue.

"Please give it up for … VALERIE!" The DJ dropped the needle on some slinky jungle jazz complete with screeches of tropical birds. Valerie brushed past me. A single yellow feather floated in her wake.

The door to the dressing room opened and Melody stepped out wearing a white satin robe covered with sparkly red roses. She saw me and laughed. "What the hell, Jack? You miss me already?" Melody's grin faltered as she noticed our faces. "What's up? Somebody die?"

"There's a man outside named Fisher. He works for a man named Anton. These guys are both bad news. They know I worked here. They might know that you and I are dating."

Melody frowned. "We're not exclusive. I mean, if you have to put a label on it —"

"This isn't the time. If they know we're dating, you're in danger."

Melody shook her head. "Damn, Jack. Why do you have to be so goddamn dramatic?"

"Come with us."

Melody laughed. It wasn't her gentle-silver-bells laugh, either. She sounded more like a pissed-off seal. "I'm at work, Jack. I got shit to do."

The bass was rattling my brain, making it hard to think. Cassandra was the primary target, but I knew Fisher and Anton wouldn't hesitate to hurt other people in their quest to get what they wanted. That meant that everyone around Cassandra — friends, parents, casual acquaintances — was now in danger.

I reached for Melody's hand. She stepped away from me, her green eyes flashing. "Get your hands off me!"

"This is serious, Mel. You really should come with us."

"Fuck you, Jack. I told you, I got shit to do."

Cassandra brushed past me. "Come on," she murmured.

Tomasso was waiting near another open door at the far side of the stage. Inside, a set of stairs led upward. I pressed my palm against the side of my head, trying to hold my brain in place. What I needed to do was clone myself. One of me could stay with Melody, and the other me could go with Cassie. Even if I could clone myself, though, I'd have to wait nine months for the clone to be born, and then it would be a baby. Maybe if there were some kind of accelerated aging —

"You coming or what?" Cassandra stood by the stairs, hand on her hip.

"Yeah," I muttered. I glanced over at Melody. She had turned her back to me. Roses and thorns chased each other across the back of her robe. *Be safe*, I thought. Then I turned and headed for the stairs.

Cassandra and I followed Tomasso up the dusty steps. The big bouncer looked down at me from over his shoulder. "You want me to talk to Bruno, get some other guys outside?"

"Nah, don't talk to Bruno." Someone had told Fisher he could find me here. My money was on Bruno. I'd have to have a little chat with him before this was all over. Tomasso nodded and kept climbing, his heavy boots kicking up dust.

At the top of the staircase was another door. Tomasso reached into his pocket and pulled out a giant brass ring of keys. He fumbled with them for what seemed like six weeks until he finally found the right one. With a click, the door swung open.

"All right, Jack. Anything else I can do?"

"Just keep your eyes open, all right?" I held out my hand again. "You did good, Tomasso."

The big man beamed, then headed back downstairs.

I pushed through the open door. Cassandra hesitated on the landing. I looked back at her. "It's okay. Come on in."

We stepped inside a big empty room. There were three small windows along one wall. The other three walls were exposed brick. Exposed pipes and ducts snaked through the rafters overhead. The wooden floorboards creaked as we walked toward a window.

I turned to Cassandra. "This used to be an afterhours joint for the high rollers. Some place to take the girls and get a drink after two a.m. A club within a club. By the morning, every flat surface in here would be sparkly with cocaine."

Cassandra raised an eyebrow. "You came here often?"

"Not if I could help it." I glanced out the window at Yonge Street. Shopping crowds, business folk, cars gliding by. Business as usual. "I don't see Fisher."

"Maybe he's around back."

"Yeah, maybe." I grimaced. "Fucking Bruno."

"He's the one that fired you, right?"

"Yeah." I peered back through the window. "It was a little misunderstanding. No big deal."

I led the way to the back of the big empty room. We went through another door and into a storeroom. More cardboard boxes lined the walls. I went over to a window and forced it open. "Let's go."

We clattered onto the fire escape. Cassandra looked down. I shook my head and pointed up.

Rooftops in the city were interesting. On a rooftop, you were in the city, but also removed from it. You could see people, but unless they were looking up, they couldn't see you. We crouched low as we scuttled across the strip club's roof.

I peered over the side into the alley behind the club. Three homeless men in tattered jeans and dirty flannel were passing around a bottle. I didn't see Fisher anywhere. "I think he left."

I turned and Cassandra was right there. Our faces were inches from each other. The wind rippled through her hair and sent long dark strands thwicking across her face. I reached up and brushed them back. We stood there for a moment on the rooftop, framed by the noonday sun.

Then she blushed and stepped back. "Jack —"

"Forget it."

"No, I mean —"

"It's okay. Let's just —"

"Okay." Cassandra stared down into the alley. Then she straightened up and smiled at me. "Let's go home."

CHAPTER 5

After all that Scotch, I kept my car keys in my pocket and left the Camry at the club. We could've taken the streetcar but we splurged and took a cab back to my office. It wasn't home, exactly, but it was close enough. We sat in the back seat together. She smelled spicy, like cinnamon and cloves.

In the old days, we would've tumbled through my office door, smashing our lips together and ripping off each other's clothes. Just the thought of it was making me hard. I flashed back to the girl-next-door brunette and her regular-sized titties snapping her G-string for the roaring crowd. I unlocked my office door and stepped inside. I needed to hobble over to the bathroom and pour a few cupfuls of ice-cold water down my pants.

Cassandra stepped through my office door and smiled. "You got a new couch."

"Yep." I didn't tell her what had happened to the old one. One night after powering back most of a bottle of

Scotch, I'd dragged the couch outside (letting it tumble down the wooden stairs with a rumble and a thud) and I set that shit on fire. I stood swaying in the alley and watched the damn thing burn. I had slept on that couch most nights, and when Cassandra and I were together, she slept on it, too. It was a tight fit, but we made it work.

Our eyes met and we both quickly looked away. Then Cassandra chuckled. "This is silly. We're adults, right? We're adults, so let's talk like adults."

Take off your top, I wanted to say. But I didn't.

She came closer to me. "You've got a girlfriend."

"Yep. Well, sort of. We're not exclusive."

"Either way, I'm not looking for a relationship right now."

"Right."

"Too much shit going on."

"Yeah. I gotcha."

"Plus our history …"

Now it was my turn to chuckle. "Who are you trying to convince?"

She blushed. "I won't lie, Jack. You're a handsome fella. You were handsome ten years ago and you're handsome now." She reached out and gently placed her palm against my chest. "Some might say even more handsome." She moved her hand away and winked. "Not me, though. You were much more handsome ten years ago."

We both burst out laughing. And just like that, the spell was broken.

I stepped toward my desk and swept some Styrofoam takeout containers into the garbage. Then I picked up a nearly empty bottle of Scotch. "Drink?"

"No, thanks." She tilted her head toward my desk. "You got a plant."

"Yep. Right after I got out of jail."

Cassandra nodded. "I heard you were Inside. What was it, a year?"

"Just under. The guy I supposedly assaulted decided not to testify."

"Where were you?"

"The Don." I poured myself a drink and drank it. "It's not a jail anymore. A hospital bought it. My old cell is probably someone's office now."

It was strange to think about — some middle manager typing away in a cubicle where I once lay on my thin prison mattress and tried not to dream. Dreaming just made things worse. If you spend all your time Inside thinking about everything and everyone you're missing, you'll drive yourself crazy. Better to tuck your head down, read some books, lift some weights, keep to yourself. When I got out of jail, I was in great shape, at least physically. Lifting all that iron and staying away from booze had sharpened my physique something fierce.

I almost died when I was Inside. A gang of cons came at me with mop handles. They would've killed me, but a guy I knew called them off. That was Tommy. He had juice because his father ran rackets on the outside. He saved my life. When I got out, I tried to return the favour. I repaid my debt, but some shit went sideways.

Cassandra stared at me. "You okay?"

"I don't like thinking about it. You know … jail."

"I'm sorry."

"No big deal. You sure you don't want a drink?"

"It's a little early for me."

"You know what they say. It's five o'clock somewhere."

Cassandra watched me pour another. "That was something I never liked when we were dating."

"What? Scotch?"

"Your drinking. You drink a hell of a lot."

"I do."

Cassandra bit her nails. "'Never turn your back on a drug.' You've heard that before, I bet."

"You don't trust me."

She paused, carefully considering her words. "It's not that I don't trust you. I know you mean well. But … you know my history with drinking."

I did. When Cassie was sixteen, she and her parents lived in Port Hope. Her home life was a mess because both her parents drank. I could relate. I never knew my dad, but my mom and all her boyfriends drank, too. One night while Cassie was at a friend's house, her parents got into a big drunken screaming match. The screaming escalated into a fight. Cassie's dad pushed her mom too hard, and she went crashing through the second-storey window and plummeted to the sidewalk. She broke her neck and died.

Apparently when the cops came, Cassie's dad was there on the sidewalk cradling his wife's broken body, rocking back and forth and sobbing, running his fingers through her long black hair. But it didn't matter. There were no do-overs. There was no going back from that. Cassie went to live with an aunt and her dad went to jail. Cassandra never talked to him again.

A sudden stillness filled my office. Cassie glanced toward the plant, its dark-green leaves straining toward the light. "I think about my mom all the time. Like, what would've happened if she had stayed in Vietnam? Would she have lived? Maybe she would've died in the war, who knows? Either way, if she had stayed, she never would've met my dad. I never would've been born, but maybe she would still be alive." Cassandra looked at me. Her eyes were wet with tears. "In Vietnam, they don't call it the Vietnam War. They call it the American War. They're still finding land mines in Laos and Cambodia. Still. Every now and then, a farmer goes into a field and *blam*."

I set my drink aside. "That's fucked up."

"Yeah." Cassandra looked around the room. "You still have your apartment?"

I shook my head. "Nope. Gave it up when I went Inside. Didn't want to pay rent and have it just sitting there."

"You could've sublet it."

"Didn't want strangers in my place."

"Fair enough." Cassandra's eyes stopped on my new couch. "So you live here, then?"

"Mostly, yeah. For the past nine years."

"Nine years of sleeping on a sofa."

"I sleep over at Melody's sometimes."

There had been other women over the years. About a year after Cassandra left me, I met Suzanne. She was a bartender in one of my favourite bars. We hit it off and then we fell in love. My world was too violent for her, though, and she left for greener pastures. I still thought about her sometimes, and when I thought of her, I wished her well.

"Right. Melody." Cassandra bit her nails. "I hope I didn't mess that up for you."

I shrugged. "She didn't want to leave the club. I wasn't going to carry her out by force." I looked over at my glass of Scotch. So tawny, so smoky. "Fisher wants me to go back tonight and meet Anton."

Cassandra's eyebrows shot up. "It's a trap."

"Yeah, probably. But we've got to talk to Anton sooner or later." I reached over, grabbed the glass and took a big sip. Almost instantly the warmth tingled through my body. "Don't worry, I won't go alone."

Cassandra smiled her crooked little half smile. "And while you're doing that … let me guess — I'll be back at the safe house watching *The River Wild*."

"It won't be so bad. It's got Meryl Streep, remember? Make some popcorn and get cozy on the couch."

"Snuggle in with Vin."

"I don't think his boyfriend would like that."

"Vin has a boyfriend?"

"Yep. His name's Carl. He sells guns."

Cassandra made a face. "You must hate that."

"I don't like guns, but what the hell." I grinned. "Anything for love."

CHAPTER 6

I don't like guns, but I do like knives. Guns are too impersonal, too imprecise. Too many innocent bystanders get killed or hurt. Knives, on the other hand, are as personal as it gets. Using a knife forces you to get in close.

I had my big Bowie knife in a sheath strapped to my chest and a smaller knife strapped around my ankle. I strapped on a third: a lightweight but deadly diving knife. Would Fisher and Anton bring friends? They would have guns for sure. There's an old saying, "never bring a knife to a gunfight," but where's the fun in that?

I dropped Cassandra off at the safe house, then headed back to the Starlight. It was around three o'clock, seven hours before my meeting with Anton and Fisher. I wanted to make sure Melody was safe and then I wanted to get her the hell out of there. She wouldn't go to the safe house, but maybe I could convince her to hang out at Eddie's casino for the night.

Bruno the manager saw me come in. A guilty look washed over his face and then he composed himself. He reached up and smoothed out his dyed-black moustache and sauntered over to me, a stupid smile plastered across his face. The dude was trying so hard to be nonchalant. I was surprised he didn't break out whistling.

"Jack! Welcome back. Can I get you a drink?"

I thought back to Cassandra's conversation. The hidden land mines still lurking beneath the surface. "No thanks. Melody around?"

Bruno looked relieved. "Sure, she's around. She's on again in about ten minutes. You sure I can't get you —"

"Hey, Bruno," I said, cutting him off.

"Yeah?"

"Next time you rat me out, I'm going to rip out your tongue."

Bruno went white. I left him standing there and walked away.

The lunchtime crowd had thinned a bit. Back to the cubicles, boys. Someone had taken away the steam trays of chicken fingers and mac and cheese. Bobby the DJ was still in his booth, grinning his cocaine grin. He did a lot of coke back when I worked here, and by the looks of it he had only gotten worse. I could practically hear his teeth grinding from here.

I wandered over to the bar. The bartender, Veronica, came over and gave me a wink. "What can I getcha, Jack?"

"Club soda."

She blinked. "With, like, vodka?"

"Not today."

She nodded slowly. "One club soda, coming up."

The bubbles fizzed into a glass. Veronica put the glass down in front of me and waited. I took a sip and slid a five dollar bill across the bar. "Keep the change."

"Thanks, Jack."

I took another sip. The bubbles fizzed on my tongue. It made me think of Pop Rocks. When I was a kid, we thought that if you put Pop Rocks and Coca-Cola in your mouth at the same time, your head would explode.

"There was a guy in here earlier — older guy, shaved head, silver goatee. I was talking to him for a bit."

Veronica nodded. "Sure."

"You ever see him in here before?"

She smiled. She had a beautiful smile. "Sorry. After awhile, they all start to blend together."

"You ever see him maybe talking to Bruno?"

Veronica grimaced.

"What?"

"Bruno." She shook her head slowly. "I like this job. I like the girls. The tips are good. But Bruno … that guy's a creep."

I waited, but Veronica didn't say anything else. "I'll talk to him."

"Nah." She flashed me her awesome smile again. "Don't bother. I can handle him."

"I'm sure you can." I took a big drink of club soda. The bubbles burned down my throat.

DJ Bobby's voice boomed from the speakers. "LADIES AND GENTLEMEN, PLEASE PUT YOUR HANDS TOGETHER FOR … MELODY!"

The crowd cheered as Melody took to the stage. She was dressed like an angel, white and radiant and glowing in the spotlight. She had a tinfoil halo and wings and everything. She was also wearing skimpy white lingerie. The lingerie wasn't exactly biblical. But then again, neither were the halo and the wings. In the Bible, angels are more like a bad acid trip. Some of them have six wings and can burn you alive (the Seraphim), others have four heads, including an eagle head and a lion head (the Cherubim), and some are wheels within wheels, each wheel covered with eyes (the Thrones). A wheel covered in eyes isn't something you'd ever want to see rolling toward you in a strip club. Or anywhere else, for that matter.

Melody was decked out like the classic pop culture angels we all know and love. She wasn't playing it cutesy, though. The look on her face as she sashayed across the stage was pure power. A challenge. *Can you handle this?*

I stood dumbfounded, watching her glow. You ever see Marilyn Monroe in *Some Like It Hot*? She glowed like that. I couldn't turn away. The bass boomed from the speakers. I stared transfixed as she shed her stockings. Frat boys hooted and cheered as she sailed her white bra out into the crowd. Then she wriggled out of her lacy white G-string. The crowd roared. Her pussy was mostly shaved, but right above her folds she had a tiny bit of blond fuzz shaped like a heart. She turned her back to the audience, giving us all a view of her smooth round ass. She looked over her shoulder, met my eyes, wiggled her wings and winked.

The frat guys were pushing and shoving each other, waving twenties in the air, everyone trying to buy a private dance. I eased my way past them. One frat boy, his face red from drinking, bumped against me hard with his shoulder. He sneered. I put my shoulder down and bumped him back. He went tumbling into his buddies. He came up snarling.

Snarling Boy swung at me. I ducked easily. The boy was drunk. I decided to walk away. The kinder, gentler Jack Palace. The boy swung again. Fuck it. I punched him and he rocked back and fell to the floor. His friends were too stunned to catch him.

Tomasso and another bouncer, Quentin, were on us like flies on shit. Snarling Boy was still on the floor. One of his buddies with thick-framed black glasses and a fascist haircut (shaved on the sides, floppy on top) was trying to lawyer-talk the bouncers, proclaiming at the top of his lungs that I was guilty of assault and they were going to sue me, the bouncers, the club, and everyone else under the sun. I looked up and caught Melody's eye. She looked pissed. Her green eyes flashed. She turned and stomped off the stage.

Tomasso helped Snarling Boy to his feet. He wasn't so snarly now. Sheepish Boy was more like it. Fascist Lawyer was still braying on about due process. I thought, *I hit the wrong guy*.

"Forget it, Carleton," Sheepish Boy muttered. "Just forget it."

The Fascist Lawyer shut his trap. The frat boys lumbered off. Tomasso stared at me and slowly shook his head. "Jack, man. Why you always gotta piss in the punch bowl?"

"Sorry about that."

I said goodbye to Tomasso and went backstage to meet Melody. Bobby the DJ was there with his mirrored sunglasses and his cocaine grin. He was leaning toward her, chatting her up. I walked right up to them and stared at Bobby. Melody turned and ignored us both. She pressed a cotton pad against her eyelid to loosen the glue of her fake eyelashes.

I kept staring at Bobby. He chuckled nervously. "It's not what you think, man. It's just, you know, when the girls sit down next to a dude and try to get them to buy a dance? The girls always pull out a scarf, right, and drape it over their seat before they sit down. It's hygienic, right? Otherwise you get girls in G-strings sitting down all over the place and the health inspector gets antsy. Anyway, what I was thinking was … what happens to all those scarves at the end of the day? Straight into the laundry, right? Well, what if, instead, we sell those scarves online?" DJ Bobby licked his lips. "Big market for stripper butt sweat. You'd be surprised. It's like how in Japan you used to be able to buy used schoolgirl panties from vending machines. Also, 'shrooms used to be legal there, too." Bobby chuckled again. "Gotta figure that's why there's cartoon monkeys and big-headed mascots and stuff like that all over the place. Cartoons everywhere, man. They've even got cartoon monkeys on bank cards. I'm telling you. Magic mushrooms, man. These days, though, 'shrooms are illegal and they yanked the panties out of the vending machines. Too bad, man. I was thinking of moving."

"So you want to buy Melody's butt scarf?"

"Hey, man, not for me. I would take it, like, on consignment. The panty sniffers buy the scarf and then Melody and I would split the cash."

I turned to Melody. "And how do you feel about this?"

Melody kept peeling off her eyelashes. "You know me, Jack. I gotta respect the hustle. But Bobby, I'll give it to you straight. You're one creepy-ass dude and I would never, ever go into business with you in a million, billion years. No offence."

Bobby's cocaine grin was unbreakable. "Hey, none taken. Just think it over, all right? If you change your mind, you know where to find me."

DJ Bobby ducked out and headed back to the DJ booth. I watched him go and turned back to Melody. "Sorry about that."

"About what? You gettin' all battle royale with my fans?"

"Yeah."

"Well, shit, Jack. It's just, you know, my livelihood."

I stayed quiet. Melody turned and looked at me. One set of fake eyelashes was gone but the other still clung to her left eyelid. "This is the part where you say, 'Oh, have you ever thought about *not* stripping, maybe you could go back to school. I have an uncle who could get you a job in the fish cannery, blah blah blah.'"

I shook my head. "I'm not going to say any of that."

Melody's eyes narrowed. "But you're thinking it."

I shot her a gentle smile. "I'm sure you've heard stuff like that in the past. But don't project what other guys have said to you onto me."

"Projection, huh?" Melody turned back to the mirror and peeled off the rest of her fake eyelashes. "You come in swinging through a crowd of fans … I don't call that projection."

"The way I see it, we're in the same business."

Melody's eyebrows shot up. "Oh yeah? Is there something you're not telling me, Jack? You moonlighting on the side?"

I shook my head. "Not like that. You provide a fantasy, I provide security. At the end of the day, we both make people feel good."

"We're in the feel-good business."

"Yeah, exactly."

Another dancer, a mousy-looking brunette whose heavy makeup didn't quite cover her bad skin, slumped over to Melody. "Hey, you got something for me?"

"Later, okay? Later."

The mouse scurried off. I stared at Melody. "What was that about?"

She arched her eyebrow. "You said it, Jack. We're in the feel-good business."

"You're selling again?"

"Look, they're going to get it from somewhere. My connect gets good shit. It's clean. The girls get their shit from me, they're not huffing bleach or who knows what the fuck else."

An old saying flashed through my brain: never ask a question if you don't want to know the answer. "Are you using again?"

"Fuck no!" Melody gave my arm a playful swat. "C'mon, man. You think I want to go back to rehab? Go through all that shit again? This is just, you know, a little side hustle. No H, just coke. No biggie. The girls party a bit, I make some extra cash, everyone's happy."

I frowned. Melody stood up and took off her robe. She was already wearing clothes: a shiny pink Adidas track suit. She saw my face and laughed. "Don't look so disappointed. You want to see me naked? You'll see me naked again real soon." Melody winked, tilted her face up to mine and kissed me. "I promise."

CHAPTER 7

I kept my eyes open as I walked Melody to the car. No one jumped out at us from the alley. I didn't see Fisher anywhere. I didn't know what Anton or the rest of his crew looked like. They could be eyeballing us right now. The meeting wasn't for a few more hours, but it was always good to arrive early, especially if there was a trap to be sprung.

I pulled a black backpack out of the trunk of Eddie's Camry. The keys to the car jingled as I slapped them into Melody's palm. Her face lit up. "Aw, Jack! You remembered my birthday!"

"Um …"

She burst out laughing. A peal of silver bells. "You should've seen your face. C'mon, man. It's not even my birthday."

"Do me a favour and drive the car back to Eddie's. Stay there, would you? Have a drink, play some blackjack."

Melody shook her head. "Not me, man. I don't gamble. Not after all that shit with my dad. Video poker, man. That shit got him hooked and no joke. He put two machines in his bar, but then he started playing that shit himself. Beep bleep boop and he just burned through ten thousand bucks. Shit, maybe more. Then one night he had enough. He was at the bar losing cash as usual and then he got all liquored up and took a fire axe to the terminals. I saw him do it, man. I was there with some friends from work. We're all there celebrating Brandy's birthday, doin' shots, you know, and then my dad comes roaring by like some kind of hell-bear, double-gripping that fire axe up over his shoulders and then WHAMMO! He busted those machines into a million pieces." Melody chuckled. "He lost a lot of business that night. Turns out when a big ol' bushy-bearded biker starts swingin' an axe around, a lot of folks run for the exits."

"Okay, no gambling. Just have a drink, then. It's on me."

Melody stepped in close and gave me a hug. Her green eyes sparkled as she looked up at me. I could see the almost invisible freckles speckling the bridge of her nose. "You're sweet, Jack. You want me to wait for you? What the hell, man. I don't have anything else goin' on tonight. I'll wait for you."

"It shouldn't take long."

"This is for whats-her-name?"

"Come on, Mel. You know her name."

We embraced, we kissed, and then Melody drove away. I slung the black backpack over my shoulder and headed for the alley.

I clattered up a fire escape and onto the rooftop opposite the Starlight. Crouching low, I made my way to the edge of the roof and peered over. Sunlight glinted off passing cars. I wiped sweat from my face and peeled off my dark-blue windbreaker. I unzipped my backpack and pulled out a pair of binoculars. I stuffed the windbreaker inside the backpack and then I hunkered down at the edge of the roof.

I was four stories up. Down below, a man in a dark-blue suit was going into the Starlight. Was he a regular? Had he ever gotten a lap dance from Melody? Mel and I were fooling around, but we weren't exactly dating. It's not like we were "going steady." We weren't sitting around the malt shop sharing a chocolate malt with whipped cream and two red-and-white-striped straws. The Starlight's door closed. I didn't feel jealous. This was Mel's job and she was damn good at it. She wasn't an object, I didn't "own" her, I had no desire to possess her and lock her away from the rest of the world like some high-grade collectible. She was a human being, fully capable of making her own decisions. I wasn't too crazy about her dealing coke, though.

I raised my binoculars and scanned the neighbouring rooftops. Nothing but pigeons. Man, that pigeon shit got everywhere. No one wants to go into a fancy store if their storefront is streaked with pigeon shit. I could always hang up my knives, go into window washing. I wasn't getting any younger. I had to make a change one of these days. But not just yet.

I scanned the street. Business as usual. On the corner, two scruffy dudes were arguing. I couldn't hear them, but their body language said it all. Eyes bulging, mouths grimacing, hands flapping, and arms waving. That was okay. The guys you had to watch out for were the ones who didn't telegraph their movements. The guys who could shoot you or stab you without so much as an eye blink. Fisher had killed people, I was sure of it. Anton probably had, too.

I only killed in self-defence. At least that's what I told myself late at night, lying in the moonlight with the shadows closing in. The booze worked for a while. Helped me sleep, helped me block out the faces of the people I had hurt and the awful things I had seen. These days, though … I would pass out and snap awake about an hour later, drenched in cold sweat, fingernails digging white crescents into my palms. That's no way to live.

I raised the binoculars again. A silver Rolls-Royce Phantom pulled up to the strip club door. The car's big front grill gleamed like teeth. The right passenger door swung open and Fisher stepped out, unfolding his lanky legs. I was willing to bet that a few decades ago, Fisher would've looked out of place next to a half-a-million-dollar car. Now, however, he had gone upscale. His mirrored sunglasses and silver goatee both matched the colour of the car.

Fisher walked around to the left-side passenger door and popped it open. I leaned forward, pressing the binoculars against my face. This was it. As long as I was betting, I was willing to bet this man was Anton. He stepped out of the Phantom and adjusted the front of his suit jacket. His suit was dark grey. His hair was black, but it looked like it was dyed. He was about a foot shorter than Fisher. His head was big and square, like the rest of him. He looked like he had been carved from a single block of granite. The strange thing was, he didn't look cruel. He didn't have an angry gleam in his eye or a mean curl to his lips. Anton was smiling. He looked happy to be out on the town, just another businessman going to a strip club with his buddies.

Fisher scanned the street and then held the strip club door open for his boss. Anton walked right in as if he owned the place. Hell, for all I knew, he did.

The driver of the Phantom zoomed away. I tucked my binoculars back into the backpack and climbed down the fire escape. I put my windbreaker back on and walked through the alley, taking my time. Breathe in, breathe out. Someone had thrown out a broken umbrella. It was half-open, five metal ribs poking straight out of a silver trash can like a hand. The umbrella looked like a drowning robot reaching out to be saved.

I waited for a break in the traffic and then I hustled across the street. I walked a block past the club and then turned into an alley. Eddie was there sitting behind the wheel of his coal-black Lexus. He rolled down the window. "All good?"

"There's at least two of them: Fisher and Anton. Maybe more inside. You?"

Eddie grinned. "All quiet on the Western Front."

I nodded. "See you in there."

Breathe, Jack, breathe. In and out. I left the alley, squared my shoulders, and headed through the doorway of the Starlight.

———

The club was bustling. It was much busier than it had been at lunchtime. The music was louder, too. The mousy dancer with the bad skin was on stage doing what looked like the twist. Her bare breasts jiggled as she danced. Her breasts were huge, all out of proportion to the rest of her body. Fake tits to a stripper were like steroids to a baseball player. Enhance your performance, get that paycheque. From this distance, you couldn't tell she had bad skin. I squeezed through the crowd toward the bar. Veronica winked at me. "Just couldn't stay away, huh?"

"You know me. I missed that smile of yours."

Her smile got wider. "You want a club soda?"

"Yeah, sure." What I wanted was whisky, but that would have to wait. I sipped my soda and scanned the room. I didn't see Anton or Fisher anywhere. They were probably in one of the VIP rooms at the back, or lurking in some dark corner, plotting and planning, figuring out when to trigger their trap. Smiley Anton didn't seem like the lurking type, though. Of course, I didn't really know the man. I saw him smile once — so what? That didn't mean shit.

I took one more sip of club soda and patted the knives beneath my jacket. No doubt Anton and Fisher both had guns. I could picture Anton smiling kindly at me while he pulled the trigger. But killing me didn't get him any closer to Cassandra. I knew that, but I wasn't sure that Anton and Fisher did.

Time to find out.

I pushed off from the bar and headed through the crowd. People saw the look on my face and got the hell out of the way. The bass booming from the speakers was like being kicked repeatedly in the chest by a mule. I glanced around the room as I walked, looking for anyone who had their eyes on me. The music was making the floor tremble beneath my feet. *Damn DJ Bobby*, I thought. I was going to shake him by the ankles until his stash of coke fell out of his pockets. Then I was going to flush it all down the drain while he begged me to stop.

Focus, Jack, focus.

Tomasso loomed in front of me, a giant column of a man guarding the entrance to the VIP room. He saw me and groaned. "Oh shit. Now what?"

"Don't get your knickers in a twist. Just meeting some folks, that's all." I peered past Tomasso's shoulder into the murk and gloom of the VIP room. Shadowy half-naked figures twisted, coming together and moving apart like the wax in a lava lamp. Men were sitting at tables with drinks in their hands and girls on their laps. I couldn't make out any faces. "Did two guys go in here? Bald guy with a silver goatee, smiley guy in a suit?"

Tomasso nodded. "Yeah, they're in there. Jack …" The big bouncer reached out and grabbed my sleeve. His face was lit up with worry. "I need this job, okay? My girlfriend's pregnant."

"Everything's fine," I lied. "Congratulations."

I stepped into the murk and gloom. Slowly, my eyes adjusted. Purple LED lights snaked around the room. I felt like I was inside a fish tank. I saw Fisher on the far side of the room. He tilted his chin at me and then turned to whisper to Anton. Anton stopped talking to the woman sitting next to him and looked at me. He smiled and started to stand.

Here we go. I headed on over. Anton, still smiling, stretched out his hand. Worst-case scenarios flashed through my mind:

I take his hand, Fisher stands up and stabs me in the heart.

I take his hand, Anton moves in close and stabs me in the heart.

I didn't want to take his hand, but I did. We shook. That was it.

"Thanks for coming, Jack. Get you a drink?"

"Yeah. Scotch."

"You got it." Anton looked at the woman sitting next to him. She was wearing a white halter top and white short shorts. Her clothes glowed purple in the LED haze. She nodded, stood up, and sashayed to the bar.

Anton gestured toward an empty chair at the table. "Have a seat."

I angled my chair so I could see both Fisher and Anton. My eyes kept flicking to their hands. That was something my friend The Chief had taught me many years ago. "Always watch the hands, Jack. They can't surprise you if you keep an eye on their hands."

The woman brought me my drink. I looked at it sitting there on the table, but I didn't pick it up. I didn't want to be poisoned. Or knocked out. Wake up in a car trunk on the way to who knows where.

Anton kept smiling. His teeth gleamed an unearthly white beneath the purple lights. "Fisher tells me you used to work here."

I nodded. "I did some security work. I wasn't a dancer."

Fisher grimaced. Anton burst out laughing. "I heard you were a funny guy, Jack. Cheers." Anton picked up his own drink and held it out.

I shook my head. "I'm not thirsty."

Anton squinted, the smile dropping slightly. Then he recovered and was once again the smilingest gangster in town. "You're cautious, too. I can appreciate that. Well, let's get right to it. We have a mutual friend. As it turns out, our mutual friend owes me money."

I nodded. "I'm here to work out a payment plan."

Anton, still smiling, turned to Fisher. "You hear that? This right here is a reasonable man." Anton turned back to me. "My associate thought you might be less than reasonable. Don't take it the wrong way. That's what I pay him for. I need someone to balance out my naturally sunny disposition."

I waited. My glass of Scotch sat on the table, untouched. I wanted to toss it back and order twelve more. I wanted to order all the Scotch. I wanted to sink deep down into a bathtub full of Scotch and stay there until this was all over. Instead I stared Anton right in the eye. "Our mutual friend says you threatened to kill her."

Anton looked shocked. Either he was the best actor in the world or the shock was genuine. "That's crazy. I don't want her dead. I just want my money. She needs to work off her debt. She can't do that if she's dead."

For a split second I pictured Cassandra dressed in Melody's Sexy Angel costume, sitting up there in heaven on a cloud, playing poker topless against a crowd of rowdy angels.

I nodded. "Agreed. But here's the thing. She doesn't want to work with you anymore."

Anton waved his arm. I caught a flash of his gold watch. It was tasteful, like the rest of his outfit. "She's superstitious, like most poker players. I can understand that. She starts working with me, she has a run of bad luck. She starts thinking I'm some kind of curse. What's the opposite of a rabbit's foot? To her, I'm like that."

"You'll get your money. But she needs her space."

Anton leaned back and sipped his drink. Fisher glared at me. "Freedom. That's what we're all striving for, isn't it? But then, we all have our responsibilities." Anton leaned forward, his eyes fixed on mine. "Certain commitments were made. Our friend needs to honour those commitments."

"You'll get your money. But she's not working with you anymore. The partnership is over."

Anton squinted. "How well do you know this friend of ours?"

How well does anybody know anybody? Under the surface, every person is a black box stuffed with secrets.

"Pretty well."

"I never threatened her life." Anton took a sip of Scotch. "She lied to you. What you need to do is ask yourself why."

CHAPTER 8

Maybe Cassandra hadn't lied. Maybe she genu-
inely felt like her life was in danger. Anton had
a well-practised smile, but just imagine Fisher looming
over Cassandra. Of course she'd feel threatened. Yeah,
but — that wasn't what she said. She said, "He threatened to kill me." Maybe it was just a misunderstanding,
a misinterpretation. Or maybe, just maybe, Anton was
right. Cassandra lied to me.

If anyone was lying, though, my money was on
Anton. Smiley Anton got up, shook my hand again, and
then walked out of the VIP room. Fisher stared at me
with those pale-grey dead-fish eyes. "Stay here for five
minutes."

This dude was really rubbing me the wrong way.
"Or what?"

Fisher sighed. "Come on, man. Work with me here.
You want to waste time exchanging threats, we can do
it. But it's been a long day. I'm going to drop Anton off at

his place and then I'm going home. You know what I'm going to do? I'm going to have a bubble bath. I'm going to put on some music, I'm going to smoke a joint, and then I'm gonna sink right down into that warm bubbly tub and I'm going to try to forget all this shit." Fisher shook his bald head. "I don't know what Cassandra's problem is. Anton helped her out of a jam and now she's trying to skip out on six hundred large? Naw, man, naw. You gotta pay the piper. When the bill comes due, you gotta man up and pay it."

"Bubble bath, huh?"

Fisher's grey eyes narrowed. "Yeah, that's right. A motherfucking bubble bath. I'm not afraid to say it. I'm telling you, Jack, that shit's relaxing. Try it, tough guy. See for yourself."

"I'm not going to sit here for five minutes. I got shit to do."

Fisher sighed again. He ran a huge hand over his shaved skull. "Let me put it this way. If Anton is getting in the car and you suddenly pop up on the sidewalk, there's going to be trouble. You want trouble? Because, personally, I could live without it."

"Sounds like you've lost your passion for your work."

"Work is work. I do my job, I get paid. You?"

"Yeah. That's about how it goes."

"Then work with me here." Without another word, Fisher turned and headed out of the VIP room's murk and gloom. Anton was waiting for him at the entrance. Tomasso was hovering near the doorway, not sure what to do. I gave him a slight nod. Tomasso stepped aside and Fisher and Anton headed out through the crowd.

The woman in the glowing halter top came over and placed a folded piece of paper on the table. For a split second I thought she was giving me her phone number. Then she said, "You need the machine?" I chuckled. Anton, that crafty bastard, had stuck me with the bill.

I slapped a few twenties into the server's hands. "Keep the change," I said. Then I headed back into the Starlight's main room.

Eddie was sitting on a bar stool with his back to the bar, taking in the hustle and bustle of the club. He saw me and raised his glass.

I walked over and joined him. "Another?"

He nodded. "Yeah, sure. How'd it go?"

I shot Eddie a grin. "I'm still alive."

"Always a plus."

I gestured to Veronica and ordered two Scotches. Eddie and I clinked glasses. Time to celebrate another day of living.

The Scotch burned down my throat like liquid fire. Warmth blossomed in my belly. Goddamn, it was good. "You saw them leave?"

"Yep. It was just the two of them. No soldiers stationed at the bar."

I sipped more Scotch. "And you didn't have to run in, guns blazing."

"Good thing, too." Eddie raised his glass to his lips. "I hate running."

"Then it was a good night."

"So what's bothering you?"

Goddamn, Eddie could read me like a book. "Anton said he didn't threaten Cassandra."

"And you believed him?"

"Yeah, I did. You should've seen his face. He actually looked offended by the idea."

"All right, so he's the only gangster in history who's never threatened anybody. What does he do, smile at people until they pay up?"

"I'm sure he's threatened people. He just said he never threatened Cassandra."

"Which means — assuming he's telling the truth, that is — that Cassandra lied to you."

I nodded.

Eddie drained the last of his Scotch. "Let's get out of here. All these naked ladies, man. If we don't leave now, I'm gonna start throwing my hard-earned money around."

We said our goodbyes to Veronica. Together, Eddie and I walked through the club's doors out into the ebb and flow of Yonge Street.

I walked with Eddie to his car. Years earlier, there was a shooting just south of here. Some gang shit that had spilled over into the streets. A fifteen-year-old girl was caught in the crossfire, got shot, and died. One minute she was out shopping with her friends, the next minute, gone. Ask me again why I don't like guns.

I eased into the Lexus and closed the door. Eddie slid into the driver's seat, reached into the centre console, and pulled out a pack of Doublemint gum. He offered it to me and I pulled out a foil-wrapped stick. Eddie pulled out a stick of his own, peeled off the foil, and popped it into his mouth. He put the car in gear and we rolled out of the parking lot.

Eddie glanced over to me. "Safe house?"

I wasn't ready to talk to Cassandra. Did she lie to me? She obviously felt threatened. Her fear of Anton was genuine.

I shook my head. "Let's head back to the ranch. Melody's waiting for me."

Eddie's left eyebrow shot up. "Melody's at the casino? Alone?" Eddie stomped on the gas.

"What's the rush? You think she's going to bust up the joint?"

"I don't know what to think." Eddie chomped his gum furiously. I could tell he was weighing his words. "I know you guys are close, but … I don't trust her, Jack."

I was quiet for a minute. "I'm not sure I trust her, either."

Eddie grunted. We zoomed south to Yonge and Dundas. These days the intersection looked like something from some crazy science fiction dystopia. Giant flashing billboards towered over the street. A little touch of *Blade Runner* here at the heart of the city. Eddie spun the wheel and we headed west along Dundas, leaving the flashing chaos of Yonge Street far behind us.

We pulled into the alley behind Eddie's building and climbed out. Downstairs, Eddie's guy Josh was manning the door. He threw it open and shook Eddie's hand as the big man walked by.

Inside the casino it looked like business as usual. No smoke, no fire. I spotted Melody right away. She was sitting at the bar surrounded by four men, a martini glass in front of her. Since when did she drink martinis?

I walked over, lowered my head, and kissed her. The men grumbled but I didn't care. "All good?"

She nodded, smiling. Her green eyes sparkled. "Everything's hunky-dory here, Jack. These guys were just explaining the finer points of poker. Whaddaya think, fellas? Am I ready to play?"

The men cheered. As a group, they started marching off to the poker tables. Melody caught my hand as she brushed past me. "How 'bout it, Jack? You feelin' lucky?"

"Another time. You have fun."

One of the Poker Bros pulled out a chair for Melody. She sat down at the green felt tabletop and grinned. "All right, gents — what's wild?"

Another Poker Bro, a serious-looking guy with greying hair and horn-rimmed glasses, frowned. "No, see — wild cards are for home games. There's nothing wild in Texas hold 'em."

"Except the bets," said another bro.

Everyone laughed. I smiled. Melody was playing dumb. She claimed she didn't gamble, but give her an hour and she would clean these guys out.

Melody played cards. Eddie and I sat at the bar and drank.

Eddie finished his rusty nail and called for another. Then he turned toward me. "You gotta talk to her, Jack."

I squinted over at the poker table. "What's she doing now?"

"No, not her. Cassandra."

"I will."

"She's not telling you the whole truth."

I sipped my Scotch. "I'm starting to get that feeling myself."

"So ..."

"I'll talk to her, I'll talk to her."

Melody came bounding up to the bar. She held up a fat wad of cash and winked. "Guess I'm just a fast learner, eh, Jack?"

I nodded. "Beginner's luck."

I eyed the four guys who had been playing poker with Melody. They glared back at me. The professor-looking guy with the horn-rimmed glasses got up and headed over to us. I set down my drink and stood up.

The Professor ignored me. He turned to Melody. "How about another game?"

"Nah." Melody grinned. "What's that they say? Quit while you're ahead."

"The fair thing to do would be to give us a chance to win our money back."

I stared at The Professor. "She said she's not interested."

"Who are you, her manager?" The Professor leered at me. "Her pimp?"

I hit him. The Prof's glasses went flying. He stumbled back, arms windmilling, eyes wide. He bumped against a table and fell to his knees. His three friends surged forward, powered by booze. Two of Eddie's guys appeared instantly, like they had just beamed down from the mother ship. The Poker Bros' courage evaporated. Eddie stood up, walked over to The Professor, and hauled him to his feet. "Time for you and your friends to go."

"He … he hit me." The Prof was clutching his jaw. Blood trickled from his mouth.

Eddie nodded. "He sure did. You can't harass women in here and expect to get away with it."

"I didn't —"

"Yeah, you did. You want to get the police involved? We all saw what happened."

"No," The Prof muttered. "No police."

"Smart man."

The Prof was smarter than he knew. Eddie wouldn't call the cops over something like this. If the situation escalated, Eddie and his guys would handle things their way.

Eddie bent down, scooped up the man's glasses, and handed them to him. The Poker Bros shuffled toward the exit.

Melody nestled up against me. That sunshine and coconut smell. "Let's go upstairs."

"Yeah," I said. "Let's do it."

Melody and I bumped through the door of my office, my ring of keys jangling in my hand as we kissed. We pushed together, her hands going lower as she fumbled with my belt. I kicked the door closed and gave her a hand, whipping off my belt and yanking down her pants. My hand cupped the front of her lacy white thong. She groaned and then let loose a little yelp as I picked her up and tossed her onto the couch. She threw her poker winnings into the air and laughed as the money rained down. I pressed my hands against her thighs and pushed her legs apart. I hooked the front of her thong with my finger and pulled it to one side, revealing her pink slit. I lowered my head and buried my face in her folds.

Melody grabbed my head and pulled me closer. My tongue went to work. After about fifteen minutes, I raised my head and yanked down my pants and boxers. I slipped inside her with one long thrust. She gasped and held on to my back. I started to move, pumping in and out. My head buzzed with alcohol and adrenalin. She felt so goddamn good.

My burner phone buzzed. *Oh shit, not now.* I pumped harder. Melody yelped. The phone buzzed again. *Shit.* I stopped and fumbled the phone out of my pocket.

"Let it ring."

"It's Cassandra."

"Let it ring!"

Fuck it. I threw the phone across the room and plowed into Melody, faster and faster and harder and harder. Her hands dipped lower, rubbing her clit as I pounded into her. She bit her lip and shook. Everything went white as I came. My body shuddered as I pumped deep inside her.

We lay together on the couch, spent. The sweat from our bodies was cooling off. There were twenty-dollar bills stuck to my legs. I started to rise but Melody grabbed on to me. "Don't go."

"I'm going to get a blanket."

"No. Just … stay with me."

I lay back next to her on the couch. She closed her eyes and breathed in and out. I brushed a stray blond hair off her cheek and gave her a little kiss. She smiled and nestled closer, her eyes still closed.

Across the room, my phone buzzed again.

Tomorrow, I thought. *Tomorrow.*

CHAPTER 9

Eddie woke me up by banging on my office door. Pale morning light was shining through the window. I shuffled across the floor, shirtless, and popped the door open. My head was killing me. I needed a little hair of the dog. I glanced back at my desk. The bottle of Scotch was empty. That was okay. Eddie had some top-notch stuff down in the casino. Of course there was no need to crack open the premium stuff so early in the morning, but then again there was no reason to drink the cheap stuff, either. I looked back at Eddie, and then I noticed the expression on his face.

"What's wrong?"

"Vin called. Cassandra's gone."

I got dressed in a hurry. I pulled on a dark-grey T-shirt and buckled up yesterday's pants. Melody sat up on the couch and rubbed her eyes. She wasn't wearing a shirt. Eddie gazed past me and stared at her breasts. She had one freckle about half an inch away from her right nipple. She raised her arms above her head, stretched, and yawned. "What time is it?"

I walked over and gave her a gentle kiss. "Eight-fifteen. I gotta go. Something's come up."

"Cassandra?"

"Yeah."

Melody yawned. "All right, baby. Get that money."

I still hadn't talked to Cassandra about money, but I could worry about that later. Melody rolled over on the couch, turning her bare back to us. Eddie and I rumbled out of my office and thundered down the stairs. Eddie lit up a cigarette as we went. "Vin woke up this morning and she was gone. No note, nothing. Her bedroom window was wide open. All her stuff was gone, too."

I nodded.

We spilled out onto the Chinatown streets and blinked in the early morning air. The fact that all her stuff was gone was a good sign. A kidnapper wouldn't have taken the time to pack. Cassandra would've been yanked through the window and that would've been that. Her stuff being gone also meant something else. I didn't want to say it. I looked over at Eddie. He took one last haul on his cigarette and then flicked it into the gutter. "Looks like she ran."

I climbed into the Lexus. Eddie followed, lowering himself down into the driver's seat. The car sank down a few inches as the big man got inside.

"Vin's still at the house?"

Eddie nodded. He patted his pockets for more cigarettes. "He feels terrible, Jack."

"It's not his fault."

"Yeah. He still feels terrible, though."

I rubbed my hungover eyes. "You don't have a flask in here, do you?"

Eddie gave me some side-eye. "It's a little early, don't you think?"

"Yeah." I rubbed my eyes again. "Fuck it. How about some coffee?"

"At the safe house." Eddie pulled out another cigarette and sparked it up. The big man put the car into drive and we sailed out of the alley.

I tried to push thoughts through my hungover brain. Shit, my phone. It was still on my office floor. Had Cassandra really tried to call last night or had that been a dream?

"Say, Eddie, let me borrow your phone."

The big man frowned. "Where's yours?"

"On the floor. Just ... can I borrow it?"

Eddie pulled one of his burners out of his suit jacket and slapped it into my hand. "Local calls only, okay?" He winked. It was a dumb joke he and I had been doing for years.

I phoned Melody. Her phone rang five times and went to voice mail. I hung up and phoned again. This time she answered. "Hello?"

"Hey, it's me. Do you see my phone?"

Melody groaned. "Man, what have you got against sleep? I mean, I don't care if you wage a one-man war on sleep as long as it's *your* sleep, you dig?"

"Sorry. My phone, though. It should be on the floor over by my desk."

"Yeah, yeah. It's here."

"Are there any texts from Cassandra?"

Silence on the other end.

"Hello?"

"Seriously, Jack? You woke me up for this?"

"It's important, okay?"

"All right, all right. Hold on." I heard a thump and a bump as Melody rolled off the couch. "Okay, checking … um … no, no texts. I have her number, though. You want it?"

"No, that's okay. I've got it. Thanks, Mel."

I could practically hear her grinning over the phone. "So, am I on the payroll now? Junior Investigator First Class. Just the facts, ma'am, nothing but the facts."

"You're hired," I said. She laughed. "Talk soon."

I hung up and punched in Cassandra's number. Wouldn't it be nice, I thought, if she just picked up the phone? "Oh, sorry, Jack. Didn't mean to worry you. Something came up, though, and I had to split in a hurry. Don't worry about Anton and the money, that all got worked out. I'll send you your fee ASAP. How's twenty percent?" Shit, as long as I was fantasizing, why not make it fifty percent? A hundred? More? "Your fee is fifty million bucks plus a unicorn and a dodo egg. Expect it all in the mail in three to six weeks."

Cassandra's phone kept ringing. It cut off before going to voice mail. The line went dead.

I passed the phone back to Eddie. "No answer."

"Sorry, Jack."

I nodded. "Wasn't really expecting one, but you never know."

Eddie thrust the phone out toward me. "Call Vin."

"What? No, man. You call Vin."

"Hey, I'm driving here. You can't drive and talk on the phone at the same time."

"Sure you can. People do it all the time."

"It's not safe, though."

"Since when are you all about safety?"

Eddie grunted. "What are you talking about? I'm all about best practices and always have been."

"All right, all right. Give me the phone, Safety Bear."

Eddie recited Vin's number. I punched it in. "Vin. It's Jack."

"Jack, man. I'm so, so sorry."

"This isn't your fault. Your job is to keep people out, not keep people in."

"I usually don't sleep like that. I don't know, man. Maybe she slipped me something."

I blinked. "You think she drugged you?"

"I'm just saying. Usually I don't —"

"Sleep like that, yeah, I got it. Were there any signs of a struggle? Any signs of another person? A cigarette butt, a footprint?"

"No, man. Nothing like that. Open window in the bedroom and the screen was off. That's it."

"Was the screen inside or outside the house?"

"Inside. It's leaning against the wall of the bedroom. You want me to put it back, or —"

"No. Just leave everything as is. We'll be there soon."

I passed Eddie the phone and we drove in silence. I didn't want to say it and neither did he, but we were both thinking the same thing. Was Vin compromised?

It seemed impossible. But then again, the king's guards were in the best position to kill the king. If someone had gotten to Vin, we were all in danger.

I glanced over at Eddie. "Should I say it?"

Eddie shook his head. "Vin? Nah. Couldn't be. Aunt Cecilia's boy? Forget about it."

"I know." We drove in silence, the engine humming, the car eating the road. "We have to at least think about it, though."

Eddie shook his head. "We're not there yet. Let's keep that shit on the back burner for now."

"Agreed."

Eddie grinned. "'Agreed.' So formal. What is this, the House of Lords?"

"Break out the robes and powdered wigs."

"Quite so, m'lord."

Just like Hawkeye Pierce in *M*A*S*H*, we were using humour as a shield. If Vin had betrayed us —

But that was a big *if*. We'd cross that bridge if we had to.

The new driveway at the safe house was really holding up. Eddie's tires bit into the asphalt as the Lexus screeched to a stop. We walked past the rose bushes to the front porch. Eddie grabbed some grocery store flyers from the mailbox. Meat was on sale.

Vin looked crushed. A sad, despondent man hunched in the front hall, his shoulder holster empty. I tilted my head toward the holster. "Where's your gun?"

"I put it down in the bathroom. I don't like, you know … the weight of it when I'm, uh …" Vin looked up. "Jack, I'm so sorry."

"I know you are, Vin. It's not your fault."

"I was the one here, though."

I grabbed Vin's shoulder. "We're going to find her. You can help. Walk me through exactly what happened. Everything since you first woke up. What you saw, what you were feeling." I rubbed my temples. "You got any coffee?"

"Espresso?"

"Make it a double."

Vin and I walked into the 1950s kitchen. Black and white floor tiles, pastel-pink cupboards, a mint-green milkshake machine on the counter. An espresso machine sat next to the milkshake machine, as if they were buddies. Vin turned on the espresso machine and got to work. "Like I told Eddie, I woke up and she was gone. I didn't hear anything, which is strange because usually I'm a light sleeper."

"The night before … did Cassandra make you a drink?"

Vin's brow furrowed as he tried to recall. "I don't think so. We had tea right before bed, but I made that. I could've turned my back on it, though. She could've easily slipped me something."

"Let's come back to that. So, you woke up …"

Vin nodded. "Went to the bathroom. Came in here and started making coffee. Made the rounds: checked the front door, looked at the street. Everything was normal. Walked through the house to the back door. Everything was fine there, too. I drank my coffee while I watched the birds. Sparrows, mostly. Then there was a flash of red. The sparrows took off and a cardinal landed on the feeder. Majestic bird." Vin passed me an espresso in a tiny cup and then he handed me a comically oversized spoon. "Sorry, the little spoons are in the dishwasher."

"That's okay." I handed the giant spoon back to him. "I drink it black. Then what happened?"

"I sat down at this table right here and read my book and finished my coffee. I went and knocked lightly on Cassandra's door. There was no answer, so I came back in here and made breakfast." Vin blinked at me. "You want some eggs?"

"Later. So breakfast is made ..."

"I went back to Cassandra's room and knocked on the door again. Still no answer. At this point, you know, I'm starting to get this feeling that something's wrong. I opened the door a crack. I said, 'Cassandra?' There was no answer. So I opened the door all the way and there was no one in the bed and the window was open and the screen was right there leaning against the bedroom wall. I ran out of the house, but it was no use. I didn't see Cassandra or her stuff. She was just ... gone."

"And then you phoned Eddie."

"Yep."

I ran my hand through my hair. I turned and walked to the bedroom. The bed was unmade. There was the screen leaning against the wall. The window was open; gauzy curtains were blowing slightly in the breeze.

I walked over to the window and peered out. I wasn't sure what I was looking for, exactly. A footprint?

A notarized map with Cassandra's current location circled in thick red ink?

I pulled out my phone and tried calling Cassie again. It rang and rang. To me, each ring sounded more desperate than the last. The phone sounded like an electric sheep bleating in my ear. I hung up and headed outside.

Birds scattered when they saw me coming. Nine in the morning and it was already warm. It was going to be a hot one. I walked around the safe house once and then I did it again. I didn't see anything. Slowly, I walked up the safe house steps. Vin was waiting for me just inside the front door. "Come on," I said. "Let's go home."

CHAPTER 10

Eddie patted his pockets, then rummaged through his desk drawer. He pulled out a red lollipop and unwrapped it. In the close confines of Eddie's office, the crinkly cellophane wrapper sounded like someone was rubbing my eardrums with sandpaper.

"What's with the lollipop?"

Eddie grimaced. "I'm trying to quit smoking. Dawn is always on my case about it. I know she's right. I bought these lollipops by the case. I know a guy who knows a guy. Got me a great deal."

"You have a lollipop guy."

"He's a wholesaler. Import/export." Eddie pulled the lollipop out of his mouth and looked at it. It glistened red under the office lights. "They're not bad. You want one?"

"Yeah, sure."

Eddie passed me a pop. He was right, it wasn't bad. I was expecting cherry, but it was more like raspberry. "So where else could Cassandra have gone?"

Eddie grunted. "She could be on Mars for all we know."

"What about friends?"

Eddie shook his head. "Cassandra doesn't have friends. She has co-workers."

I stared at Eddie. "When Cassie and I dated, I never met any of her friends, either."

Eddie shrugged. "Some people don't have a lot of friends. It's not a crime."

I stood up. "If Cassandra ran, she'll need cash. She'll be looking for a game."

"Assuming she's still in the city."

"Gotta start somewhere."

Eddie rolled his lollipop to the other side of his mouth. "There's another question you should be asking. If she ran, what's she running from?"

I went back up to my office. Melody was long gone. I caught a whiff of her perfume as I walked past the couch. I picked up my phone. There were the two missed calls from Cassandra. No texts, no voice messages. She had tried to call me last night. To warn me? To ask for help? To say goodbye? There was no way to tell.

I heard a floorboard creak. I froze. I wasn't alone.

I pulled a knife from beneath my jacket.

The bathroom door handle turned. I heard a chuckle. I stepped to the side of the bathroom door and waited. A man stepped out of the bathroom, spotted me, and nodded.

I nodded back. "Hello, Grover."

The man standing in my office was about five foot two and maybe ninety-eight pounds. He had sandy-brown hair, a brown moustache, and half-glasses perched on the edge of his nose. He was wearing white slacks and a pale-lemon cardigan. He was also the deadliest man I had ever met. I once saw him slit a man's throat with a playing card. I hadn't seen him in nine years, not since that mess with Tommy.

Grover smiled. "Do me a favour, would you, Jack? Put that thing away."

I stared at him. I knew enough not to ask how he got into my office. I slid the knife back into its sheath. "This isn't a good time."

"Let's see if we can fix that. Drink?" The little man walked over to my desk and poured me a drink of my own Scotch.

"Seriously. A woman's gone missing. I have to find her."

Grover nodded. He passed me the glass and poured another for himself. "Sounds like you're keeping busy." He sipped his drink and grinned. He looked like a shark. "This won't take long. I need some cash, Jack. About a hundred grand should do it."

I shook my head. "You caught me at a bad time, money-wise."

Grover frowned. "You wouldn't be holding out on me, would you, Jack?" Grover walked over to the window and peered down at the street below. Then he looked over his shoulder, back at me. "Call it a loan. I'll have it back to you — with interest — in no time."

"Grover, I'm telling you, you can't get blood from a stone. Maybe your friends in Florida …"

Grover grimaced. "We didn't really have friends in Florida. We thought we did, but those assholes sold us out. We had to run. Marguerite, you know, she's not from our world. She got freaked out and left me."

I blinked. "I'm sorry."

Grover shook his head. "Don't be. It was a long time coming. We were together for eighteen years. No matter how you slice it, that's a big chunk of time."

I pictured Grover's wife floating in a deep expanse of blue, her eyes wide open. Grover laughed. "Don't look like that. Marguerite and me, we're still friends." Grover shrugged. "Whatcha gonna do, right? These things happen." He took a sip of Scotch and grinned at me. "How about you? You doing all right?" Grover tilted his chin. "You got a new couch."

"Like I said, this isn't really a good time."

"Who's the woman? Maybe I can help."

I shook my head. "Nah. Thanks, though."

"You could put me on the payroll. How much is this woman worth to you?"

"No, it's ... it's not like that."

Grover ran his hand through his thinning hair. "Marguerite got almost everything in the divorce, Jack. Her lawyers sniffed out accounts I didn't even know I had. I've got some ideas, but you know what they say. 'It takes money to make money.'"

"You know I'd help you if I could."

"That's what I thought. After everything we've been through, surely I can count on Jack. That's what I thought."

My phone rang. Grover and I looked at each other. "Well? You going to answer that?"

It was Melody's number. I kept Grover in my sight as I walked, trying to create some distance between us. "What's up?"

"Jack! I'm at my dad's bar. Remember that guy from the club?"

"Anton?"

"No, the other guy. The big biker." Melody lowered her voice. "He's here."

CHAPTER 11

Walking into The Bull was like stepping back in time. Neon beer signs, big clunky wooden chairs and tables, the musty-bar smell of stale beer and old smoke. You couldn't smoke indoors anymore, but other than that not much had changed since the 1970s. The men at the bar were older and greyer. A jukebox was playing "Fortunate Son" by CCR.

Melody gave me a big bear hug. I hugged her back. Goddamn, she smelled good. She smelled like coconut lotion and the beach. She smelled like summertime. "Fisher's out back having a smoke. Come on, let's go see my dad."

Without waiting for an answer, Melody grabbed my hand and pulled me toward the bar. A stocky, bear-like man with shoulder-length wavy grey hair stood scowling behind the bar. "Dad, this is Jack. Jack, this is my dad, Walter."

Melody's dad grunted. I wasn't exactly a meet-the-parents type of guy, but I figured I could fake it. I stuck out my hand and Walter shook it. His grip was strong, but not walnut-crushing. Some guys shake hands like they've got a lot to prove. Walter didn't. This was his castle and he was the king.

The old biker watched my face. I tried to look trustworthy. I leaned closer to Walter. "I'm looking for a man named Fisher."

Walter grunted. "You a cop?"

"Come on, man. Do I look like a cop?"

Walter gave me the once-over. "Yeah. Yeah, you do. A little bit."

"It's the hair, isn't it?" I ran my fingertips across the close-cropped side of my head.

"The hair, yeah. And you got this … I don't know, man. You got this cop-like intensity about you."

"I'm actually a pretty easygoing guy," I lied.

Melody frowned. "Jesus Christ, Dad, come on. He's not a fucking cop."

"All right, all right." Walter squinted. "Fisher, huh? Yeah, I know him. He and I used to ride with Satan's Blood back in the day."

"Do you know a man named Anton?"

Walter's eyes narrowed. "What the fuck, man? You want me to make you a list of every motherfucker I know? Because let me tell you right now, I know a lot of motherfuckers."

"Dad!"

"No. Something ain't right." Walter squinted. "Too many damn questions, man." Walter turned his back to me, came out from behind the bar, and stomped toward the back door. He cracked it open and glanced out no less than four times before he stepped outside.

I could understand Walter's paranoia. You don't get to be his age in his line of work without being pretty damn careful. I followed the old biker outside. Fisher was standing in the parking lot smoking a cigarette. I watched as Walter talked to Fisher and pointed back at the bar. Fisher looked back at me and frowned. He flicked his cigarette to the ground, climbed onto his bike, strapped on his helmet, kick-started his Harley, and roared away.

I walked over to Walter. The old biker narrowed his eyes. I gestured at Fisher. "Tipped off your buddy, huh?"

"I got nothing to say to you, man."

Fisher doubled back. The motorcycle dipped as he raised a gloved hand wrapped around a pistol.

Shit.

I ducked as the gun went off. Fisher squeezed off three shots and then he screeched around the corner. My knife was in my hand, though I didn't remember pulling it out. The sound of Fisher's engine grew fainter and fainter. He wasn't coming back for a second pass.

I turned to the old biker standing next to me. His face was white. "Walter?"

Walter opened his mouth and blood spilled out. The old biker crumpled to the ground.

I had picked up some first aid over the years, but I couldn't tell how bad he was hit. There was a lot of blood. Elevate, I thought, lifting up the man's head. I pressed my hand to his bloody stomach. He groaned.

Walter clutched my arm with surprising strength. "Tell Melody I love her. Tell her."

I nodded. "Just hold on. You're gonna be fine." The words rang hollow in my ears. Walter's blood was seeping through my fingers. Other people were gawking now, poking their heads through restaurant doors and gathering in the parking lot. I shouted, "Call 911!" *Just another responsible citizen. Don't mind me, folks.*

I knelt on the asphalt, hands pressing down on the bleeding man. The ambulance came. It didn't take long. But then, my sense of time was fractured. I backed off and let the paramedics do their thing. They got Walter strapped to a gurney and hustled him into the ambulance. It rolled off, siren screaming, painting the street with flashing lights. I stood there with my hands dripping blood and watched them go.

CHAPTER 12

I hate hospitals. I mean, no one jumps up and down and claps their hands and shouts "Hooray! The hospital!" Don't get me wrong, the doctors and the nurses and the clinicians and the porters and everyone else who works in a hospital to save lives on a daily basis are goddamn heroes. And there are plenty of grateful folks out there who think kind thoughts about the hospitals that have helped them out over the years. Like my buddy Eddie.

Eddie makes sizeable donations to SickKids Hospital every single year. His daughter Dawn had an intussusception when she was two years old. I'm not talking about the Leo DiCaprio movie with the spinning top. Intussusception is bad fucking news. Part of little Dawn's intestine had slid into another part, just like collapsing a telescope. This can cut off the blood supply and kill the tissue of the intestinal wall, which can then cause a rip in the intestines and lead to peritonitis, which can kill you dead. Luckily, Eddie got Dawn to the hospital before any of that happened. The docs at SickKids re-inflated her intestines and she pulled through. The annual donation was Eddie's way of saying thanks.

In the hospital cafeteria, Melody looked so small, sitting hunched at a table, dwarfed by the enormity of her surroundings. She had a big steaming bowl of minestrone in front of her. She had told me she wasn't hungry, but I figured she should probably eat something. The soup was untouched.

Melody looked up at me. She looked like she had been up all night trying to put together a jigsaw puzzle using pieces from a hundred different sets. "Seriously, Jack. What the fuck?"

I reached out and took her hand. "Shit's fucked up."

"Yeah. No shit." Melody sighed and dragged her spoon through the soup. "Sorry. I didn't mean to snap at you. It's just — my goddamn dad." She shook her head. "When I was a kid, I never thought he would get shot. He and his buddies had guns and lots of them. I didn't think anything of it, you know? The way you grow up is the way you grow up."

I munched on an egg salad sandwich. It tasted exactly like nothing. Plain grey mush. "I'll be right back." I stood up and carried the sandwich over to the condiment station. The sandwich was my patient and I had to doctor it up. I loaded it up with salt, pepper, and Tabasco and took a bite. *Doctor, we're losing him!*

I forced myself to take a few more bites — the body needs fuel — and then I chucked the soggy mess into the garbage and walked back to the table.

Melody pointed to my empty hands. "What happened?"

"I'm sorry, Melody. The sandwich didn't make it."

Shit, Jack, what kind of fucked-up joke was that? Melody's dad was shot and you're cracking wise about not making it? Goddamn, man!

Still … was that a smile? A slight uptick of the lips, and then it was gone. Melody turned her face to the window. The moonlight was streaming in. "My dad used to make sandwiches for my school lunches. My favourite was cream cheese with grape jelly, with the crusts cut off." Melody smiled. "You should have seen him back then, Jack. This big, tough, long-haired, big-bearded biker, covered in tattoos, walking little six-year-old me to school, hand in hand. I'm sure the other parents and teachers didn't know what to make of him at first. But you know what? He was there. He came to every soccer game, every school play, every recital. He volunteered on field trips. He took me and my friends to the ROM and he would pretend to talk to the animal exhibits. He would do the animal voices, too. 'Hello, Mr. Polar Bear, how are you today?'" Melody made her voice gruff, imitating her dad imitating a bear: "'I'm fine, how are you?'" Melody smiled at the memory, her eyes welling up with tears. She dabbed at the corners of her eyes with a paper napkin.

"After my mom left, he was my dad and my mom. You know? I didn't think it was anything unusual. It was just my life. But he wasn't like the other dads. It wasn't just because he was a biker. Just being that involved in your kid's life back then, as a dad … that was different.

The other dads were more distant. I remember one of my friends, Claire. I'd play at her house and her dad would serve us milk and cookies with a towel draped over his arm, acting like he was a waiter at a fancy French restaurant. Later he went to jail on some stock fraud shit. But mostly it was the moms. All the other moms would make a big fuss over me. Claire's mom once sent me home with a big lasagna. I thought it looked delicious, but my dad ... you should have seen his face. He was so angry he was shaking. He literally turned red. 'She thinks I can't feed my own kid?' He had his Satan's Blood jacket on, the one with the big grinning, bleeding devil on the back. He was going to go over to Claire's house and, I don't know, throw the lasagna in Claire's mom's face or something. I was clutching on to his arm and screaming, begging him to stop. He had been drinking ..."

Melody looked down at her soup. "Eventually he calmed down. He didn't go over there and he still let me go play at Claire's house, but he didn't let us eat that lasagna. It looked so good, too." Melody scooped up some soup. "This isn't bad. You want some?"

"Yeah, sure."

Quietly, we shared the soup.

CHAPTER 13

Walter was wide awake, sitting up in his bed in the ICU. There was a giant white bandage taped to his stomach. A short nurse in light-blue scrubs with yellow happy faces on them was bustling about, checking the lines that snaked into Walter's skin.

Walter saw us and frowned. "Can you believe this shit? They're not letting me eat. I'm fucking starving."

"You got shot in the stomach, Dad."

"Yeah, well — I'm not going to get better if I can't eat. Ain't that right, Matilda?"

Matilda the night nurse shook her head. "Can't eat just yet, Mister Walter."

Walter grinned at us. "Bullet missed all the vital organs. Another inch, it would've shattered my spine." He turned slightly and winced. "Still hurts like hell. Where's that goddamn morphine button? Is this thing even on?" Walter looked up at me. "Goddamn placebo is what it is. A dummy button. You click and click and click and you're still getting the same tiny dose."

"Otherwise you'd OD, Dad."

"Don't give me that OD shit. I've been doing drugs since before you were born. Matilda! I need some fentanyl up in here. Come on, help a brother out."

Matilda made a *tsk tsk* sound and hustled away. Walter leaned back against his pillows. "They've still got to sew me up some more, reconnect some veins and shit." He stared at me and narrowed his eyes. "Right after you came to see me, I get shot in the gut. That's what I call a crazy fucking coincidence."

I stepped closer to Walter and sat down in the chair next to his bed. "I assume you're not going to call the cops."

Walter looked at me like I had sprouted a second head.

I nodded. "You want to work it out yourself, that's fine with me. You and Fisher can work it all out. But, see, there's other people involved in this." I turned halfway in my seat and pointed to Melody. "We have to keep her safe."

Walter grimaced. With a grunt, he heaved himself closer to me. His eyes flashed with anger. "You think I can't protect my own daughter? Get the fuck out."

"I didn't —"

"I SAID GET OUT!"

In the hallway I closed my eyes and took a breath. *Breathe, Jack, breathe.* On the other side of the door I could hear Melody talking to her father in low, measured tones. That's it. Get the old man to calm the fuck down.

A porter with dyed-black hair and huge Elvis-style mutton chops strode past me, pushing an old lady on a gurney. The lady was twisted and tiny, about the size of two watermelons laid end to end. She reminded me of the most predictable headline in the world: World's Oldest Person Dies. Who could've seen it coming?

Two young doctors who looked like they were about twelve years old walked past going the other way, laughing like they didn't have a care in the world. Melody walked out into the hall, passed the doctors, and fell against my chest. I wrapped my arms around her. "It's going to be okay."

"He wants me to bring him his gun." She laughed and wiped away a tear. "Shit."

I didn't say anything. I hoped Melody knew she couldn't bring a doped-up man a loaded handgun. If he started firing at shadows during the night, those stray bullets could hit anyone.

Melody looked up at me. "He's scared, Jack. He'd never admit it, but he is. Shouting at you, that's his way of showing it. Men like him, his generation, they weren't taught to feel. All his life he's been told to 'suck it up' and 'be a man.' Anger's become his only go-to emotion."

"Or maybe he's just an asshole."

Melody laughed. "Yeah. Well, he is that." She glanced back into the hospital room. Walter had turned his back to us. He was muttering under his breath and jabbing at the morphine button with his thumb. "Who shot him, Jack?"

I hesitated before answering. "It was Fisher."

Melody shook her head. "It doesn't make any sense. Everybody loves my dad." She shot me a sad little smile and walked back into Walter's room.

I was willing to bet that Fisher hadn't been gunning for Walter. He had been gunning for me. Walter was just an unlucky bastard who had been in the wrong place at the wrong time.

I lingered in the hallway with my ear near the door, trying to overhear Walter and Melody's conversation. Walter's Mumble Game was strong. I couldn't hear shit.

I walked down the hall until I found a pay phone. I dropped in my coins and dialled up Eddie. "Any word on Cassandra?"

"Nothing yet. Got a line on someone she used to play cards with, but they haven't called back yet."

"Keep me posted." Quickly I filled Eddie in about Fisher and Walter. "I think he was gunning for me."

"That's fucked up."

"What can I say? The man is high strung."

"Speaking of which … did you hear? Grover's back in town."

"Yeah, I heard something about that."

"Watch your back, Jack."

I hung up the phone. Apparently payphones are filthy germ factories just swarming with all kinds of creepy-crawlies. Makes sense if you think about it. When was the last time you saw a janitor pick up a pay phone and give it a good wipe-down?

I stood alone in the hospital hallway, listening to the chirp and ping of distant machines. And that's when it hit me. There wasn't going to be a pot of gold at the end of this rainbow. There weren't going to be any soaring strings, sunlight bursting through the clouds, or angelic choruses. Best-case scenario: I was going to find

Cassandra, help her pay off Anton, and then she would go back to her life and I would go back to mine, and that would be that.

But then again, as my old friend The Chief used to say, ain't nobody got a crystal ball.

CHAPTER 14

I missed The Chief. The man had saved my life. I had bombed out of school, left whatever was left of my family far behind, and I was drifting, aimless, until The Chief found me.

"I recognized something in you," The Chief told me years later as we sat on the deck of his trailer watching the sky turn pale pink with sunset. The Chief was smoking one of his foul home-rolled cigarettes that dyed the skin of his fingers formaldehyde yellow. The man had hands like a preserved corpse.

I didn't smoke. I was sitting back on one of The Chief's ratty old plastic chairs sharpening my knife, dragging the blade back and forth against the whetstone. "Oh yeah?" I said, scraping the knife against the jet-black stone. "What's that?"

I thought he was going to say something encouraging, some Hallmark card sentiment about Stick-To-Itiveness or something of the sort. Instead he smiled, the stubble around his cheeks more salt than pepper. The sun kept dipping down, turning the sky from pink to deep purple, the colour of a bruise. "When I looked at you, I saw myself."

The Chief's body was never found. Sometimes, even though I know better, I think maybe he's still out there somewhere, living it up on a beach in Antigua, wearing swim trunks and a billowing white shirt, a frozen margarita in his hand, his bare feet toasted brown by the sun. The Chief was gone, though. He wasn't coming back. Sometimes that's what happens. Not everyone lost gets to be found.

CHAPTER 15

Eddie clapped me on the back and sat down next to me on his stool at the end of the bar. The casino was in full swing. He held up two fingers to Vivian, the bartender. Viv nodded and gave him a wink. She pulled Eddie's private bottle of Scotch out from under the bar and poured two fingers into two glasses. Then she slid the Scotch across the bar to us.

I gave her a smile. "Thanks, Viv."

Eddie and I clinked glasses and drank. Goddamn, it was good.

"How's Melody?" he asked.

"She's doing okay. Her dad was lucky, man."

Eddie's left eyebrow shot up. "Getting shot in the gut counts as lucky now?"

"You know what I mean. He could be paralyzed. He could be dead."

"True, true."

I leaned closer to Eddie and covered my mouth with my hand. Time to play The Mumble Game. "Grover was here earlier, in my office. I didn't let him in. Did you?"

"What?" Eddie looked like I had just slapped him upside the head. "You know I didn't."

"That's my point. Somehow he got in here. I want to check the security tapes."

Eddie sighed and drained the last of his Scotch. "I've got a thousand bucks that says the tapes won't tell us shit. Grover's gonna Grover, man."

"Yeah, well, I want him to Grover somewhere else." I finished my Scotch and stood up. "I'm going back to the safe house. Maybe there's something I missed."

"You need to sleep, Jack."

"Fuck that. She's out there somewhere."

"You'll find her when she wants to be found." Eddie stretched his hands up over his head and yawned. "That guy I was telling you about? Used to play poker with Cassandra? He says he'll meet."

"Great. Let's go."

"Tomorrow, Jack. Regular people sleep at night."

The body needs rest and the body needs fuel. I knew this, in theory. Putting it into practice was something else.

I was never an easy sleeper. Plunging into my own mind every night was not something I looked forward to. I thought maybe sleep would come easier as I aged, but if anything, it was getting worse.

I left Eddie down in the casino and went up to my office. I unlocked all the locks and then I slowly swung the door open. I flicked on the lights with my left hand and pulled out my knife with my right. Slowly, I reached over to the bathroom door and jerked it open. The bathroom was empty.

One of the benefits of having a tiny place is that it doesn't take long to search. No one was hiding in the bathroom or behind the couch or underneath my desk. I put my feet up at the desk, poured myself a whisky, and raised my glass to my plant. "Salud."

I was hoping the whisky would shake something loose from the ol' brain pan. Something I had overlooked about Cassandra.

The first drink didn't do it, so I poured a second.

Cassandra, Melody, Walter, Fisher, Anton, Grover. I needed one of those conspiracy corkboards with the thumbtacks and the red thread. Get all the players up on the board, see how they connect. I rummaged through my top desk drawer. I had some thumbtacks somewhere, I was sure of it. First though, one more drink.

"Rise and shine, Sleepyhead."

I groaned. At some point in the night I had made it over to my couch. Eddie stood filling the doorway. I resisted the urge to hurl an empty bottle at him.

"Go away."

"Come on, bud. Get up." Eddie grinned. "Time to see the Cowboy."

CHAPTER 16

The one-eyed man peered through the curtains, rifle in his hands. "Damn coyotes. They come up from the ravine and eat my peacocks."

I looked over Cowboy's shoulder at the wide expanse of lawn gently sloping down to the Rosedale Ravine. A garden party was in full swing. Servers in formal attire carried silver trays of canapés through the crowd. A beautiful brunette with long tan legs and short white shorts was trying to convince a man in tan slacks and a yellow sweater to play croquet with her. She had him by the arm and was pulling him toward the wickets. *Just do it, you fool.*

I didn't see any peacocks. I tilted my chin toward the lawn. "Sorry for taking you away from your party."

The one-eyed man shook his head. "That's my wife's scene, not mine. She loves this shit. If I went down there, she'd make me break out my formal eye patch."

Right now Cowboy wasn't wearing an eye patch at all. The place where his eye had been was all pink and puckered and scarred. Eddie had told me the story. In his younger days, Cowboy had been heavily into various substances. One afternoon while high on PCP, he had gone on an epic biblical trip that ended with him shrieking, "If thy right eye offends thee, pluck it out!" Which he did. Goddamn PCP, man. That's some horrible, horrible shit.

I nodded toward the rifle. "Is that thing loaded?"

Cowboy frowned. "Wouldn't be much good otherwise. What am I going to do, jump through my window and club a coyote to death?"

I grinned. "I bet you could if you had to."

He laughed. "You're damn right." He leaned the rifle against the wall and stepped toward the bar. "Drink?"

I nodded. "Scotch. Something smoky." I glanced around, taking in the tapestries, the fireplace, the floor-to-ceiling bookcases. "Nice place."

"Ah." He dismissed it all with the wave of his hand. "Got lucky, that's all. Invested my money in the right shit at the right time."

"Simple as that, huh?"

"Well ..." Cowboy's eye twinkled. "There was the small matter of getting the money to invest in the first place."

I nodded. "Speaking of which ... you still know some people from the old days, right?"

Cowboy shook his head. "I put all that street shit behind me. You know what I'm into now? Music. I've got my own studio down in the basement." He grinned. "Want to see? I'm working on some killer tracks, man."

"Another time. You know why I'm here."

Cowboy nodded. "Cassandra."

I nodded back. "That's right."

He exhaled. "Yeah, I knew her. Man, that was like a million years ago. I staked her in a few games. Nothing too crazy, you know. A million, tops." He laughed. "Like I said, man, that was a long time ago."

"You know a guy called Fisher?"

The one-eyed man paused for a minute, tapping his chin. "Fisher. Yeah, sure. He was a road captain for Satan's Blood. Those guys were stone cold killers, but man, they could really move the shit." Cowboy chuckled. "It's funny, you know? With all the shit I made, the acid was the best. We're talking world-class quality. Fisher and his crew never fucked with it, though. They wanted meth. As much meth as I could cook. For a year I had a lab out on an island up north. I'd fly up there every weekend on my float plane. I was hiding garbage bags full of meth all over the damn place. Under rocks, inside tree stumps, you name it. When I got back the next weekend, the shit would be gone." He shrugged. "They sold it mostly in the States — Florida, Louisiana. The Southern Pipeline. The meth goes south and guns come back north." As Cowboy smiled, the skin puckered up around his missing eye. "They were the ones who gave me the name Cowboy. I don't know why they called me that, man. I've barely even seen a cow." He scratched his arm. "What's Fisher been up to? Last I heard, he was still locked up."

"He's out now. He's tight with another old-timer named Walter. They rode together back in the dinosaur days."

"Walter, Walter … yeah, sure. Big guy, long frizzy hair like whatshisname … Richard Simmons."

"The workout guy?"

"No, wait. The guy from KISS." Cowboy rose unsteadily to his feet. "Gene Simmons. You want another drink?"

That was another problem with booting around the city in a borrowed car. You'd have to be a fucking idiot to drive drunk.

"Coffee."

"Coffee? I can do coffee."

The coffee was bitter as hell, but I drank it anyway.

"Do you know a man named Anton?" I asked.

Cowboy closed his eye, and when he opened it, he squinted at me like he was seeing me for the very first time. I had the feeling he'd been hitting the sauce pretty hard before I arrived. "So, Jack, here's the thing. I don't know you. Don't get me wrong, it's been real nice to stroll down memory lane and all. But these people … it's been years. Decades. The only reason I agreed to meet you is that Eddie said you're a stand-up guy. I got a nice little life here. I busted my ass to carve this out. Cassandra, yeah, sure, we played cards, I staked her. We had some laughs and made some money. I haven't talked to her in years. I don't know anyone else. You understand?"

CHAPTER 17

I left Cowboy's Rosedale mansion and drove north on Mount Pleasant. The name of the street was no lie. This part of the street was surrounded by parkland. It was like driving through a tunnel of trees.

I cut west on Inglewood, up to St. Clair East. A little bridge took me over the park and the creek that ran through it. I continued west on St. Clair. The parks dropped away and the city rose up. I drove across Yonge, past streetcars and skyscrapers. I used to know a woman who lived around here. Silvia. We spent one hot summer drinking sangria and getting naked on her balcony. She loved showing off her body, her curves in all the right places. I was usually a little more private, but fuck it. That summer was so hot and the sangria was so damn sweet.

I turned off the AC and rolled down the window. Cowboy had dummied up quick when I brought up Anton. There was something there. I just wasn't sure what.

At the hospital, I stopped at a kiosk and bought two giant coffees.

Melody was sitting outside her dad's room, hunched over her phone. She looked up at me with bleary red eyes. I passed her a coffee. "You get any sleep?"

She tucked her phone into her purse and wiped her nose with the back of her sleeve. "Not much."

"How's he doing?"

Melody slowly nodded. "He's a tough old bastard. Still wants his gun, though."

"I think he's safe. I don't think Fisher was trying to shoot him. I think he was gunning for me."

Melody sipped her coffee and stared straight ahead. "See, I'm not sure about that. Fisher and my dad, they've known each other for a long time. They had some kind of falling out. I think it was about the coke." I waited for her to continue. She didn't, though. She just sat in the hospital hallway, clutching her giant coffee with both hands.

"What coke?"

She sighed. "My dad moves a little product, you know, on the side. He's not Pablo Escobar or anything. A few weeks ago, his shit got jacked. Home invasion. Two robbers burst on him late at night when he was drunk off his ass. They had shotguns and were wearing clown masks, like those rubber ones that go over your whole head, with the curly red hair and everything. They forced him to sit his ass down in his ratty old cigarette-burned La-Z-Boy, and then they tore out that fake 1970s-style wood panelling in his basement rec room until they found the stash — four kilos of a hundred percent pure uncut coke."

"Where does Fisher come in?"

"It was his shit. Fisher and my dad were working it together. Fisher blames him for his shit getting jacked. At least, that's what my dad thinks." Melody sighed again. "You know they both rode for Satan's Blood, right? They had this crazy scheme that they were going to bring back the Blood. Boom down the highway with their colours flying, 'Glory Days' by Springsteen pumping from the speakers. The coke was supposed to finance that. Fisher got a good deal on some shit and my dad was supposed to move it. They take the cash, buy some new bikes, get some recruits … it's crazy, right?"

"Your dad told you all this?"

"Shit, he wouldn't shut up about it. Blah blah blah Satan's Blood blah blah blah." Melody set down her coffee, smoothed out her pants, and stood up. "I need a cigarette. You coming?"

Outside, a summer storm was blowing in. The wind was whipping the trees. The sky was the colour of dirty dishwater. Melody popped a cigarette in her mouth and rummaged through her giant purse. I pulled a lighter out of my pocket, stepped forward, and lit her cigarette.

"So Fisher thinks Walter stole his cocaine."

"That's about it." Melody sucked down smoke. "It's not my dad's fault. Sometimes shit just goes sideways, right? Act of God and whatnot."

"Who do you think stole the coke?"

Melody shook her head. "Shit, man, I don't know."

"They knew where he hid the shit."

"Maybe. Or maybe they jammed a shotgun under his chin and said 'Where's the shit?'"

"I need to talk to your dad."

Melody lifted her head toward the dishwater sky and blew a perfect smoke ring. "Later, okay? He just came out of surgery. He's a tired old man, Jack."

"Fisher might've kidnapped Cassandra. Your dad might know something about —"

"Uh-uh. No way. My dad doesn't know shit about any kidnapping."

Lightning flashed. I rubbed my head and tried to think. "Fisher's coke got snatched. He needed money. Cassandra was making money for Fisher's boss, Anton. At least until her luck went south."

"You really think she ran out of luck?" Melody finished her cigarette, dropped it on the sidewalk, and ground it out with the heel of her sneaker. "I think she was just sick of the gig, man. Being trotted out to play poker with a bunch of mobsters. She probably wanted to get back to the nice quiet days of taking down the marks at Casino Rama. Shit, she's probably there right now." Melody jerked her thumb toward the hospital doors. "I'm going back in. Call me later, okay?"

"Wait. How do I reach Fisher?"

"He's sweet on one of the girls at the club — Janelle. Little mousy girl, bad skin." Melody shrugged. "Try her. She might know."

CHAPTER 18

The cab smelled like burnt plastic. Janelle and I drove straight up Bathurst, past Bloor, past Dupont, past Davenport. Right before St. Clair we veered left and continued north on Vaughan Road. We passed the Dutch ice cream shop, the janitorial supply store, and the occult shop. My ex, Suzanne, bought a candle in there once that supposedly was a "money-drawing" candle. You light it up and money starts sticking to you like a magnet. In her case, maybe it worked; she got a gig in Saskatoon and moved away.

We kept driving north toward Oakwood. Janelle pointed out the window. "That's the house."

The cabbie started to slow down.

I said, "Keep driving." Then I turned to the woman sitting next to me in the back seat. "Thanks again, Janelle."

She smiled. "Anything for Melody."

We drove past slowly and checked out the house. From the outside, it didn't look like anything special.

Just another quiet bungalow on a quiet street. There was a tidy hedge and a cherry tree in the front yard. The cabbie pulled over down the street. I paid him, and Janelle and I headed back to the house.

There was an old brown Ford station wagon in the driveway. A few scraggly flowers pushed past the weeds in the planter bed at the front of the house. The concrete porch steps were starting to chip away. If Fisher had money, he was hiding it well.

On the front door was a big red-and-white sign that said OXYGEN IN USE. Someone in there had medical problems and was using an oxygen tank. I knew what the sign meant: don't come strutting into the house puffing on a stogie like Winston Churchill. But I suppose you could put up a sign like that in any house where someone was breathing. Hell, yeah, I use oxygen. My plan was to keep using oxygen for as long as I could.

I turned to Janelle. "What's with the oxygen sign?"

"Fisher's Mom, Daisy. She's ... not well."

Shit, I thought, *Fisher's mom?* She must be a hundred and ten years old.

I knocked on the door. No answer. I knocked again, a little bit louder. Still no answer. I peeked in past the OXYGEN IN USE sign. I could see into the living room, which was cluttered but clean. There were at least four clocks in there.

I thought about going around back, but I didn't want any neighbours getting squirrelly and calling the cops. If Fisher wasn't home, I could always come back. Borrow a car from Eddie. Camp out in the car and wait. Get a Thermos full of coffee, some sunflower seeds, and an empty two-litre bottle to piss in. What more could a guy want?

The blinds flickered. Someone was there, peering out. The blinds flickered again and the face disappeared. Janelle frowned. "Fisher is suspicious as hell. He thinks everyone from the milkman on up is wearing a wire."

"The milkman? What year is this? Is your old man living in a *Heathcliff* cartoon?"

"A what?"

"You know, Heathcliff? The cat that wasn't Garfield?"

Janelle stared at me blankly. I shook my head. "Forget it."

We sat in the gloom of the living room. The clocks tick-tocked. An old German shepherd thumped its tail against the floor. Fisher smoked his cigarette and sipped his beer and tilted his head toward the dog. "Came back from the vet today. Cost me two grand I don't have." The biker shrugged. "Maybe I'm a fool, but I can't just let him die."

"What's his name?"

"Brutus." The old dog's ears perked up at the mention of his name. Then, slowly, they deflated back down against his skull. Brutus looked at me and growled.

I kept my hands where they were. I knew better than to try to pet a biker's dog.

Fisher looked over at Janelle. "Take Brutus downstairs, will you? Me and Jack need to talk." He reached into his pocket and pulled out a bone-shaped biscuit. The old dog creaked wearily to his feet. His tail thumped on the floor. Fisher tossed the dog biscuit in the air. Brutus clumsily lunged for it, and the biscuit hit him on the nose and bounced onto the carpet. The old dog took a step forward and gobbled it up.

Janelle stood in the living room doorway. "Brutus, come!"

The old dog looked over at his master. Fisher nodded. "Go on."

I watched them go, then I turned to Fisher. "Did you try to shoot me?"

Fisher smiled. "Son, if I tried to shoot you, you'd be shot."

"Where's Cassandra?"

Fisher stared at me. He took another pull from his cigarette. "If I knew that, you think I'd be wasting my time sitting here talking to you? We're looking for her, too."

"I heard about your scheme with Walter. Bringing back the Blood. That's some ballsy shit. That's going to piss off a lot of people."

"You mean the Angels? Anton's got connections there. He's gonna smooth it all over."

"I think you're dreaming. Worse, I think you're caught in another man's dream."

Fisher slammed his fist against the table. "Bullshit! Bringing back the Blood is my baby."

"I heard you had a little problem with the seed capital."

Fisher narrowed his eyes. "I don't know what the fuck you're talking about."

"The coke. I heard it got ripped off."

"You heard, huh?" Fisher ground out his cigarette in a skull-shaped ashtray. "Fucking Walter. He talks too much."

"Is that why you shot him?"

Fisher shook his head. "Walter and me, we go back years, man. We'll work it out."

I leaned forward. "If you and Walter go against the Angels, that's your funeral. But if you've somehow gotten Cassie involved in this …"

Fisher shook his head. "That's all Anton. She owes him money and she skipped. If she's still alive, we'll find her."

"If she's still alive?"

"I'm just saying, man."

I stared at Fisher. "Why did you suggest meeting here at your house?"

"You think I'm scared of you?" Fisher shook his head. He lit another cigarette with his silver Zippo. "I'm not scared of you."

I tilted my chin at Fisher's cigarette. "You're smoking in a house full of oxygen tanks. One wrong spark and the whole place goes up."

"Oxygen tanks don't work like that."

"That shit is flammable."

"Nah. It's non-combustible." Fisher shrugged. "It is an accelerant, though. Oxygen makes small fires bigger. Like using a bellows on fire in a fireplace." He stared at me. "My mom's tanks aren't going to blow up in some badass movie-style special effects explosion. If someone lights up a smoke while wearing an oxygen mask, they could scorch their face. That's about it." Fisher frowned. "Dynamite, though. That's a different story."

"You've got enemies."

"We've all got enemies." Fisher took a puff from his cigarette. "You and I, we don't have to be enemies. I invited you into my home as a show of trust. Some people you can't trust at all. You, though, I don't think you're going to dynamite my mom."

"Aw shucks. What a nice thing to say."

Fisher grinned, flashing his gold tooth. "You're a joker. I like that about you. Some of these guys, it's all tough guy, blank face, thousand-yard stare, no matter what's going down. They think being tough means blocking out their emotions. I say fuck that. Feeling is tougher than not feeling." Fisher took another drag from his cigarette. "Course, some of these guys … they can't feel. Some of them are straight-up psychopaths. You dig?"

I nodded. "I've met my share."

"Yeah, I bet you have." He stared at me. The clocks tick-tocked. "I'm not a psychopath," he added.

"Good to know."

"Anton … well, I'm not going to talk shit about my boss."

"You're a good soldier."

"Damn right." Fisher ground out his cigarette in the skull-shaped ashtray. "You and me, Jack, we got something. You know what that is? Soul."

The man was drunk. This was some real I-love-you-man type shit. "Just like Sam & Dave," I said.

"No, not like Sam & Dave! I'm not saying we're gonna hit the stage with matching sequined suits and bust out all kinds of awesome dance moves. I'm saying you've got heart." Fisher patted the pockets of his jean jacket. "Damn. You got a smoke?"

"Sorry. Quit years ago."

"Smart, man. That nicotine gets its hooks in you, no joke." Fisher stood up and bellowed, "JANELLE! You got any smokes?"

I heard Janelle's footsteps as she came up from the basement, then a skittering of paws as Brutus followed her up. Silently, looking away from Fisher, Janelle handed him a pack of cigarettes. I frowned.

"You want a beer? Janelle, two beers. What the hell, get one for yourself, too."

I didn't like the way Fisher was talking to his old lady. That stupid, old school, macho, mean-to-women bullshit was played out. Janelle silently left the room and headed for the kitchen. Brutus stumped over and curled up at Fisher's feet. He reached down and scratched the dog behind the ears. "So, I trust you. Trust is a rare thing. I'm reaching out, man. You and me, we want the same thing. We want to find Cassandra. We want her back safe and sound." Fisher leaned back into the couch grinning. "I say we work together."

"What do you think, Janelle?" I smiled at the mousy woman, who was lingering in the doorway, three beers in her hands. "Should Fisher and I work together?"

Fisher frowned. "Why the hell you asking her?"

Janelle flinched. She didn't look at me when she answered. "If it helps find this woman … then, yeah, sure. Why not?"

"All right," I said. "I'm in."

CHAPTER 19

Maybe working with a biker who had the habit of shooting his friends in the gut wasn't the smartest idea I ever had, but if it would help me find Cassandra, then I was willing to give it a try.

I stood in Walter's hospital room and listened to the machines ping. The big biker was looking better. Bushy-tailed and rosy-cheeked. He was sitting up and smiling at me. "They say I can go home today."

"That's great."

"You talked to Fisher?"

"I talked to him. He says shooting you was a misunderstanding."

Walter grunted. "He's a hothead, that's his problem. Add a few beers on top of that — it's a volatile combo, man."

Melody bounced into the room. "Knock, knock! You ready to go? The nurse is getting a wheelchair as we speak."

"I don't need a fucking wheelchair."

"Come on, Walter," I said. "Take the free ride."

Melody held out her hands. "Okay, Dad. I'm going to help you up. You ready?"

Walter winced, rolling over in his hospital bed. The hospital sheets crinkled like paper as he rolled. He grabbed on to Melody's wrists. "One, two, three, PULL!"

Melody heaved her dad out of bed. I stepped forward to help stabilize the old biker. Walter looked over at me and frowned. "See, what I'm worried about is Fisher coming back to finish the job."

"He wants his coke or his money. Give him that and you're square."

Walter coughed. Melody handed him a tissue. He hawked up a giant green loogie and folded it into the tissue. Walter shook his head. "I should have never brought him into this deal in the first place."

"Fisher says bringing back the Blood was his idea."

Walter barked out a laugh. "Yeah, right. Fisher's a soldier, Jack. He does what he's told. Bringing back the Blood, that's some big-picture shit. That's all me." The old biker turned to me and winked. "You ever ride?"

"Sometimes."

"There's nothing like it, man. That feeling you get when you're on the open road and you're with your brothers, hundreds of 'em, stretching out as far as the eye can see, and the engines are growling and the sun is shining and the countryside is blurring by …" Walter smiled. "You can't top it."

"So why didn't you patch over?"

The nurse came in with the wheelchair. Melody and I helped ease Walter into it. Melody glanced at me. "Can you push him? I'll bring the car around."

I pushed Walter down the hospital hallway. An orderly passed us, pushing a giant cart loaded with trays. Feeding time.

"Those guys that patched over ... you know what they made them do?"

"No, what?"

"They had to burn their colours, man. All the Satan's Blood jackets, hats, bandanas ... they had to toss all their stuff into a burning oil drum. They didn't have to get beaten in, though, and they got to keep their tattoos." Walter rolled up his sleeve. There on his bicep was the classic bleeding Satan logo: trickles of blood pouring from Satan's grinning mouth and eyes. The tattoo was done in jailhouse blue. I had seen similar tattoos when I was Inside. One guy on my cell block, Nestor, was a whiz with a modified tattoo needle made out of a ballpoint pen and parts of a sewing machine. Walter thrust out his jaw. "I wasn't about to burn my colours, man. Not then and not now. Satan's Blood for life."

CHAPTER 20

The inside of Fisher's station wagon smelled like coffee and cologne. One of my mom's boyfriends had a car like this. His name was Jerry, and he was one of the nice ones. He would let me go "fishing" in the vinyl seats, wiggling my little hands into the spaces where coins had dropped out of Jerry's pocket. I got to keep whatever I found. One time I found a stick of spearmint gum still wrapped in foil, and I got to keep that, too.

Fisher sipped his takeout coffee and twisted the dial on the ancient radio. Sweet soul music came trickling from the speakers. Ray Charles, "What'd I Say." Classic. Fisher reached over and turned down the volume until the music was almost subliminal. "Your coffee all right?"

It was too sweet for me. "Yeah, it's fine."

"I wasn't sure how you took it."

I took a sip. "It's fine."

"All right, Jack. The way I figure it, Cassandra played fast and loose with Anton's money, and when it came time to pay the piper, she skipped out on the bill. That sound about right?"

I frowned. The sugary coffee was hurting my teeth. "We were working on a payment plan, though. She came to me to help broker the deal."

"Payment plan. Yeah, right. Six hundred grand at a dollar a day. She'd be fully paid off in only one thousand six hundred and forty-four years. Her descendants could leave that shit on Anton's grave."

"Not a dollar a day. We're working it out. You were there at that meeting."

"I'm not sure what meeting you were at because I remember that shit differently. Seemed like you were taking Cassandra away from Anton, and Anton didn't like that shit."

"Anton and Cassandra, that's done. He needs to realize that."

"It's not done. She's going to play again and she's going to play for Anton." Fisher took a big sip of his coffee, reached forward, and fired up the station wagon's engine. The car coughed, then started up. "All we need from her is one last big game. Make all the money back and then she can waltz off into the sunset."

Fisher cranked the wheel and the old brown car slid into traffic.

"One last game. What if she loses?"

"I don't want to hear that glass-half-empty shit. Go into a game thinking you're gonna lose, guess what, you're gonna lose." Fisher drove with his left hand, clutching the coffee in his right.

I was beginning to think that maybe Cassie would be better off if we didn't find her. If she was safe, then maybe she should stay hidden, wherever she was. But then, if she was safe, then why hadn't she phoned? Why wasn't she picking up?

I took another sip of the too-sweet coffee and turned to Fisher. "Cassie's hand. You know the story there?"

Fisher grunted. "Yeah, I know the story. You have to understand. Anton ... he's a volatile guy. Sometimes he goes too far."

"He burned her."

"They were in a hotel room. She was boiling water for tea. He was pissed that she was losing. He grabbed her hand and forced it down deep into the kettle."

"Jesus."

Fisher spun the wheel. The car veered right. "A few years back, Cassandra came to us for help. We helped her and then she started playing with Anton's cash. At first it was great, but then her luck went south." Fisher shot me a sideways glance. "I'm not excusing the man, but he was frustrated. Six hundred grand is no small change, man."

My giant hands curled into fists. My knuckles were white and my nails were digging into my palms. "Fuck the money. You don't treat a human being like that." I wanted to find Anton and I wanted to hit him until he was dead. "Where's Anton now?"

"Cool your jets, Jack. He shouldn't have burned her, I agree. That shit was horrific. But put that shit out of your head. I know you can't, but try. I got a line on Cassie."

I stared at the big biker. Fisher looked straight ahead through the windshield. "Anton got a call the other night. This guy that used to work for us, Johnny Rapoli, he was calling to see how much Cassandra was worth to us."

My fists tightened. They were bartering Cassie like a side of beef. Cassandra, the woman I once loved.

"He's got her?"

"He didn't say. He said he knows where she is." Fisher grimaced. "He runs a dog-fighting ring out near Orangeville." Fisher shook his head. "Those poor dogs, man."

"Let's go see Johnny."

Fisher nodded. "Rapoli rolls heavy. You ready for that?"

I cracked my knuckles. "I'd like to phone a friend."

CHAPTER 21

I met Grover in a French restaurant on Baldwin Street. He looked up and smiled as I came through the door. The little man was sitting, as always, with his back to the wall and with a clear view of the door. He was wearing a pale-yellow cardigan and granny-style half glasses that were perched on the tip of his nose. A *Globe and Mail* newspaper sat on the white tablecloth in front of him, and next to it was a glass of white wine. I gave him a nod and we shook hands. I sat down and pointed to the newspaper, which was folded open to the business section. "You looking for another line of work?"

Grover chuckled. "You know what they say: 'You can rob more people with a pen than you can with a gun.'"

The server glided up to our table with a smile on her face. She had long black hair pulled into a ponytail and big silver hoop earrings. I blinked. She looked a lot like my ex, Suzanne. She was looking right at me. I stared back. Grover nudged my arm. "She said, 'What do you want to drink?'"

"Oh. Uh, a coffee. Black. No sugar."

The server slipped away. Grover took off his glasses and flipped the newspaper closed. "What's up?"

I ran it down. Cassandra, Fisher, Walter. I kept my words jailhouse vague — the restaurant was busy, there were a lot of ears to overhear — but Grover knew what I was talking about. The little man whistled when I was done. "Damn, Jack. I'm always impressed by the way you can step in shit wherever you go."

"What can I say? It's a skill."

The server returned with my coffee. I thanked her and took a sip, then watched as she moved away. I wondered what Suzanne was up to in Saskatoon. I hoped she was happy.

I glanced back at Grover. "I've got a line on who's holding Cassandra. Johnny Rapoli."

Grover shook his head. "Doesn't ring a bell."

"Runs a dog-fighting ring up near Orangeville."

Grover's eyebrows shot up. "When are we going?"

"Tonight. Fisher's coming with us."

Grover frowned. "I don't trust him, Jack."

"That's because you're smart."

We left the restaurant and walked toward Grover's car. We drove without talking. The suspension on Grover's dark-green Lexus was so smooth that the car seemed to float along above the road. Quiet jazz trickled from the speakers. Grover smiled. "Next time I go down to

Florida, you should come with me, Jack. Get out of the city for a while."

I nodded. "Yeah, maybe." Leaving the city. It sounded impossible.

"Don't get me wrong, I love the city. But it's important to step out every now and then. Clears your head. Gives you a fresh perspective." Grover reached over and turned up the radio. "Listen to this. New John Coltrane. They thought these recordings were lost, but then they turned up. They released them just last year."

I listened to the squawking horns. Lost and then found.

"Rapoli's not going to give her up easily."

"Thing is, Jack … it's all in how you ask."

CHAPTER 22

Johnny Rapoli screamed as Grover broke another finger. That was the full five. In the background, Johnny's dogs were barking. I stood by the doorway of Johnny's shed. He had come down the driveway to meet us. When he saw Fisher's motorcycle, he'd tried to run, but Fisher cut him off. I'd jumped out of Grover's Lexus and tackled him to the ground.

Johnny glared at us. "You're fucking dead. Do you know who I am?"

Grover hit Johnny with the butt of his gun. "You're a fucking asshole who likes to hurt animals. Did I get that right?" Grover hit him again.

Johnny spat blood onto the floor. One of his teeth bounced on the concrete.

I stepped forward. "Where's Cassandra, Johnny?"

"Don't know any Cassandra."

Grover hit him again. "Wrong answer."

"Okay, okay. A buddy of mine, he's got her."

I slapped my burner phone on the wooden table in front of Johnny. "Call him up."

Johnny Rapoli shook his head. "He's not gonna pick up if he doesn't know the number."

"So use your phone."

"I don't have a cellphone."

Grover blinked. "What are you, a caveman?"

Johnny jerked his head. "Land line's in the house."

Grover levelled the gun. "Okay. Let's go."

Our boots crunched through the gravel as he headed for the house. The dog kennel was behind the house to our left.

Johnny broke and ran.

"Shit!" Grover popped off a shot.

"Where'd he go?"

Fisher whipped out his gun. He squinted in the darkness. "See, man, this is why we should do this shit in the daytime."

I cocked my head. "Listen. You hear that?"

Fisher frowned. "All I hear are those poor goddamn dogs."

Grover looked toward the kennel. "Wait. I hear it, too."

Beneath the sound of the barking dogs, a woman was screaming.

I turned and ran for the kennel.

"Jack, wait!"

Gunfire pinged off the gravel. I kept running, heading into the gunfire, zigzagging toward the kennel.

Fisher threw himself down next to me. The old biker was panting heavily, trying to catch his breath. "Motherfuckin' Charge of the Light Brigade. Gonna get us all killed."

Fisher raised his gun. I caught his arm.

"There's a woman in there with him. Maybe it's Cassie. We can't just fire blindly."

Grover ran toward us, clutching his right hand. "Shit! Shit, shit, shit. I'm hit. That sonofabitch shot me."

I tilted my chin. "Let me see."

Grover took his left hand away. I leaned in close to see. Blood spilled from his right hand.

"Shit."

Grover pulled out a handkerchief and winced as he wrapped it around his hand.

"Keep the pressure on."

"I know, I know." Grover's mouth was a thin grim line. "Let's get this motherfucker."

We ran for the kennel. Fisher got there first and kicked down the door. We all ducked to the side as gunfire rattled out. Then we ran in.

Fisher got off the first shot. Johnny Rapoli spun around. Grover shot him again. Johnny dropped his gun. I stepped forward and kicked the gun, hard. The pistol skidded across the concrete floor and vanished into the shadows.

I ran past the cages. The dogs snarled and threw themselves against the bars. On the other side of the cages was a small storage room. There was a woman tied to a chair beneath a single bare bulb. She looked up. Cassandra. I knelt down and she burst out sobbing. "It's okay," I said, knowing that it wasn't. "It's okay."

I pulled out my knife and cut Cassandra free. I helped her back past the cages. The dogs kept barking. Cassandra buried her face in my chest.

Fisher stepped forward and Cassie recoiled. "You're safe," I told her. "He's not taking you back to Anton."

The old biker nodded. "Not tonight."

I turned back to Cassie. "Wait for us outside."

"No." Cassandra clutched me tightly. "I'm staying with you."

"You don't want to see this. Please. Go outside."

She looked into my eyes. Then she nodded.

I watched her go, and then I turned and punched Johnny Rapoli as hard as I could. I hauled Johnny to his feet and tumbled him into an old wooden desk chair. The man sat there, slumped and bleeding, struggling for breath.

Grover stared at him. "Johnny, Johnny, Johnny. Didn't your mother ever teach you not to shoot people?"

Grover raised his gun. Johnny thrust out his bloody hand. "Wait!"

Grover looked over at me. I nodded. "Do it."

Grover pulled the trigger. In the close confines of the kennel, the gunshot was incredibly loud. All the dogs went nuts, barking and howling.

We left the kennel. Fisher reached for Cassie, but again she recoiled. I helped her limp along the gravel driveway toward the vehicles. With his left hand, Grover dug into his right pocket and fished out his car keys. "Here, Jack. You drive."

Fisher strode past us and straddled his Harley. "Someone's gonna have to tip off the cops. Otherwise all those poor dogs are going to starve to death in their cages."

I stared back at the kennel. The dogs were still howling. "I'll do it." An anonymous call from a lonely roadside payphone.

I helped Cassie into the passenger seat of Grover's Lexus. Grover climbed into the back seat and pulled a first aid kit out from under the seat. He stuffed gauze into the bloody hole in his hand. "Rip off some of this tape for me, would you, Jack?"

I ripped off a long piece of tape and passed it back. Grover taped up his hand.

I turned to Cassandra. She was slumped down in the passenger seat. "Are you hurt?"

She stared at me. Her eyes were blank. "Let's just go."

I nodded. Yeah. There was a doctor I knew in the city, someone who did work off the books for the right price. I put the car in drive and we headed down the driveway.

Cassandra screamed. Johnny Rapoli was standing in the driveway, blood pouring from his empty eye socket. Johnny staggered forward and raised his gun.

I stomped on the gas and slammed the Lexus into Johnny. The man vanished beneath the wheels. Then I threw the car into reverse. I felt the tires bump over Johnny Rapoli's head. Cassandra screamed again. Tears were rolling down her dirty face. I slammed the car into drive and stomped on the accelerator. The tires spun on the gravel and then we rocketed forward. I caught a glimpse of the grey boards of the kennel in the side mirror. What was left of Johnny Rapoli lay jumbled in the driveway. His twisted body grew smaller and smaller in the rear-view as we headed back to the city.

CHAPTER 23

Grover and I sat in the waiting room of Doc Warner's Yorkdale office. As underworld doctors go, she was one of the best. Grover's hand was covered with fresh gauze. He shook his head. "Jesus. How 'bout Johnny staggering around like that with a bullet in his brain? That was some real *Walking Dead* shit right there."

I closed my eyes. I could still feel the thump of the car tires as they ran over Johnny's head.

Doc Warner walked out of her operating room and snapped off her latex gloves.

"How is she, Doc?"

"Physically, she's fine. A little dehydrated, but that's an easy fix. Mentally, though ..." The doc shrugged. "That's a different story."

Doc Warner turned to Grover and held up a tiny piece of mangled metal. "You want to keep the bullet?"

Grover grinned. "Sure, why not? I'll turn it into a keychain or something."

I walked over and knocked on the door of the operating room. Cassandra's voice sounded muffled and small. "Come in."

She was sitting on a small two-seater couch. I went over and sat down next to her. She turned away. "I'm an idiot, Jack."

"Don't blame yourself."

"I got scared and I ran. I tried to phone you."

"I know."

"I checked in to a hotel and then I found a poker game." Cassandra looked away. "Rapoli was there." She turned back to me, eyes flashing. "I won that game, Jack. I beat them all. And then they wouldn't let me leave."

"I'm sorry."

Cassandra stared straight ahead. "You ever get that feeling that the walls are closing in?"

I nodded. Cassandra continued. "A few years back, I was in a bad place. Anton helped me out." Cassandra hung her head. "I didn't know who he was. But now I do. He's a real sack of crap. I had to get out of there." She tugged down on her right sleeve, trying to cover up her burns. "Anton wouldn't let me leave. He said he owned me, fair and square." Cassandra burst out sobbing. I reached for her, but she pulled away. She took two deep, shuddering breaths. "I was an indentured servant. I had to pay him back. I had to go where he told me, play poker with who he told me to. At first it was okay. I was winning. The chips were stacking up. And then it all went south."

"Your luck changed."

Cassandra frowned. "I don't believe in luck. It's all about context. Life moves, Jack. It flexes and twists. It's like a snake. You slip and fall and break your leg. Bad luck, right? But then the next day someone tries to draft you into a war. You can't go because your leg is broken. Same leg, same break, only now it's good luck rather than bad."

"Context."

"Yep."

Cassandra reached over to a box of tissues on Doc Warner's table and pulled one out. She wiped her eyes and blew her nose. "I had to get out of the safe house. I could hear Anton and Fisher scratching at the door. Not, you know, literally. But they were out there and they were going to find me."

"We'll work it out."

"Six hundred grand is a lot of money, Jack."

"Sure. Now it is. In a couple hundred years, after inflation, that'll be the price of a chocolate bar."

Cassandra smiled her cute crooked smile. "That doesn't help me much, though. In a couple hundred years, you and I will both be bones."

I stood up. "We're alive now, though. Let's make it count."

CHAPTER 24

"**S**o she's back?" Melody snuggled up to me on her couch.

Cassandra was at this very minute back in my office on my couch trying to sleep. "I feel safe here, Jack," she'd said.

I nodded. "We got her back."

"So, when's the big payday?"

"I don't think that's how this works."

Melody pulled away. She looked at me, puzzled. "What do you mean?"

"I'm doing this as a favour. I don't think there's going to be any money."

Melody blinked. "Let me give you a refresher, Jack. You work, you get paid. That's how it works."

"It's not always about money."

Melody stared at me. Then her face softened. "No, you're right. I've turned down paying gigs before. Did I ever tell you about The Rattler? He's a regular down at the club. We call him The Rattler because he always wears this hat with a snakeskin band. A few years back, he offered to buy me for a year — put me up in a luxury apartment, pay all the bills, get me a new car, whatever. I was flattered, you know? Don't think I didn't think about it. Maybe if he'd been better looking. But that dude always smelled like sour milk. He was the type of guy who probably had a bunch of taxidermied elk heads nailed up all over his house. That shit's creepy, man."

"How old was he?"

"I dunno. Sixty? Sixty-five?"

"And you were, what? Twenty? Twenty-one?"

"Twenty, yeah."

"That's fucked up."

Melody shook her head. "Nah, I don't think so. Older men have been sniffing around me my whole life. Started when I was eleven. This contractor working on the house next door propositioned me when I was coming home from school. It didn't stop there, either. Older men — like, guys in their thirties, forties — looking me up and down at the mall, the library, wherever. Teachers 'accidentally' brushing up against my breasts or my butt. Guys grabbing my ass on the bus, driving by whistling, shouting all kinds of vulgar stuff." Melody puffed and exhaled. "That's life, right? When I was with my dad and his crew, that shit was squashed. I felt safe. And then I got a little older and there was this one guy, Patches. Yeah, I know, funny, right? Bad-ass biker with a name like a cat. Anyway, he started coming on to me real gentle-like, you know, not vulgar or anything. I was fifteen. He was twenty-seven. I was flattered, you know? Thought I was real mature. Thought I was special. This cool older guy, taking an interest in me ..." Melody shook her head. She reached forward and ground out her cigarette in the ashtray. "It was all consensual, but looking back on it, it was a little fucked up, you know? Like, at fifteen, I thought I was hot shit, but I was just a kid. That dude was almost thirty. I mean, what the fuck, man?"

"I'm sorry."

Melody shook her head. "Don't be. It is what it is. Men have been looking at me my whole goddamn life." She grinned. "Now they just have to pay for the privilege."

The doorbell rang. Melody looked up. "Hold on a sec." She kissed my cheek and bounced to her feet. I watched her leave and then I stood up and followed.

A tall young man stood with Melody in the kitchen, which was trapped in the 1970s — shitty yellow and brown linoleum floor and wood panelling everywhere. Melody was always griping about how she was going to remodel one of these days, but she hadn't done anything about it yet.

Melody grinned. "Jack, this is Marcus."

Marcus and I shook hands. His grip wasn't strong. The man looked worried.

"Marcus and I have a business proposition for you. You want a beer?"

"Yeah, okay."

Melody popped open the fridge and pulled out three beers. "Here's what we're going to do. You know I've been dealing now and then at the club, right? A few bags here and there, no biggie. Well, we're going to up our game. We've got some coke, and we're gonna step on that shit and then we're going to rock it up. And Marcus here is going to help sell that shit."

Marcus frowned. "You didn't say anything about crack. I don't know shit about selling crack." He shook his head. "That's racist, man."

Melody frowned. "Come on, Marcus. You know it's not like that. It's not because you're black. It's because you've got the connect. You've got plenty of steady customers lined up with their hands out."

Marcus shook his head. "My people want powder, man. I sell to friends at parties, friends of friends, a few folks I know in the restaurant biz, and at school. I'm telling you, I don't know shit about crack."

Melody scowled. "We'll figure it out."

"Seriously. Powder, that's where it's at. This one dude from the suburbs, he drives in and gets it for his wife. Or he says it's for his wife anyway." Marcus dumped a baggie onto the coffee table and chopped out a line. "You want some, Jack?"

I shook my head. "Coffee is more my speed." I looked over at Melody. "So you're moving up the ladder?"

Melody fiddled with the fringe on her purse. "I'm tired of all the penny-ante bullshit. We're expanding the operation." Melody grinned. "We got a lot of shit to move and we're gonna move that shit fast. Get the money and go."

Marcus nodded. "That's what I'm talking about. See, I'm saying we wholesale the shit. What the fuck, right? Retail or wholesale, it's all pure profit to us."

I frowned. Melody shook her head. "See, that's your problem right there. When faced with an easy hundred grand or a hard million, you choose the easy hundred."

"I'm just saying, there must be guys around who would take that shit off our hands in a heartbeat. Someone with connections we don't have."

Melody snorted. "Connections? *You've* got connections. *I've* got connections. I've got the market cornered in that fucking club. When I started, there were all kinds of skeezy guys slinging bullshit bags of baking soda and baby laxatives. I came in there with your shit, and within two weeks the girls were practically eating out of my hand." Melody scowled. "But you know the bosses have to get their beaks wet. I got to kick back some cash to the managers to have them look the other way. They walk off with the profits while I'm in there busting my ass doing all the work."

I nodded. "Capitalism in action."

"Yeah, well, I got no problem with capitalism. We've just got to get ourselves higher up the food chain."

I drank my beer. "You do that, you're going to start bumping into the competition. What happened to those skeezy guys at the club?"

Melody shrugged. "I kicked up more to the bosses. They made the other dealers go away. But I hear ya, Jack. We need some muscle." Melody grinned at me. She raised her eyebrows. "That's where you come in."

I shook my head. "You've got the wrong guy."

Melody gave my arm a swat. "What the fuck, man? You allergic to money? We got a good thing going here."

"How does it play out now? Like if someone doesn't pay. What do you do?"

Melody nodded. "We've dealt with deadbeats before. The way it works is, Marcus and I go over to their houses with baseball bats. And then we go shopping. We take DVDs, CDs, clothes … whatever we want. Last time I got an Hermès scarf."

"A scarf, huh?" I kept watching Melody's eyes. "Have you ever used the bats?"

Marcus shook his head. "It's an intimidation thing."

"No one's ever called your bluff?"

Melody scowled. "It's not a fucking bluff. They don't pay, they WILL get the bat." She stared over at Marcus. "Okay? Rock that shit up!"

"What do I know about running a stash house?"

Melody frowned. "Man, I don't know. Make the shit and then stash it. C'mon! Stop making it harder than it has to be. I've got to go to work. Just get it done!" Melody stood up and flounced down the hall. We heard the front door slam.

Marcus looked over at me. "Look man, we could really use some help here. I mean, I sell to friends, co-workers, people I trust — but we're talking an eight ball here, an eight ball there." Marcus rubbed the side of his head. "But this shit, I mean, damn. It's going to take us a million years to move that kind of weight."

I stared at Marcus. "What did you mean, 'either way it's pure profit?'"

Marcus squirmed. "You know, I'm just saying, either way we make money."

"Pure profit means you didn't pay for it."

"Shit, man."

"Melody ripped it off." I didn't want to believe it but I knew it was true. "She stole her dad's coke."

"I don't know anything about that."

"She knew where her dad hid the shit and she went right for it. You were there, too, weren't you?"

Marcus didn't say anything.

"You need to give the shit back."

He shook his head. "We can't. You heard Melody. She's got big plans."

I kept staring at Marcus. "A lot of people are going to get hurt behind this shit. Give it to me and I'll give it back to Walter, no questions asked."

Marcus chuckled. "You think I'm dumb, huh?"

"I don't think you're dumb."

"Yeah, right. I'm not gonna let you just waltz off with our coke, man."

"But it's not your coke. Melody ripped it off. She stole it from her father, who got it from a man named Fisher. Fisher works for a man named Anton. These guys are bad news, Marcus. You think they're going to let you walk off into the sunset with their shit? Hell, no. They're going to come looking for it."

Marcus looked worried. "For real?"

"As real as it gets." I shrugged. "But why are you worried? You got bats, right?"

CHAPTER 25

I left Melody's house and hopped on the Queen street-car heading west, back toward Chinatown. At Queen and Spadina, I decided to walk the rest of the way to my office. It was a beautiful day.

A man in a long white butcher's coat was stacking bok choy in a big pile outside one of the big Chinatown markets. An inch of ash dangled from his cigarette. I watched for a while to see if the ash would fall onto the vegetables, but it never did.

I knew I would have to confront Melody about her dad's stolen coke. She and Marcus were in way over their heads. Walter might let his daughter slide, but Marcus was a different story. Plus, there was no telling what Fisher would do.

Speak of the devil. Fisher was parked outside my office, lounging back on his chromed-out Harley. The big biker was wearing a black leather jacket and mirrored sunglasses. He grinned when he saw me coming. "She's up there, isn't she?"

"She's still pretty shaken up. She doesn't want to talk."

Fisher nodded slowly. "That's cool. I don't want to, you know, disturb her. But you and I, we had a deal."

"Deal's still on. Anton will get his money."

"He wants her to play, Jack."

I shook my head. "That part's done."

Fisher sighed and looked off into traffic. I could see the reflections of cars in his sunglasses. "He's not going to be happy about that."

"Just keep reminding him about the money. He still makes a profit on the whole deal." I flexed my fingers. I imagined my hand closing around Anton's throat.

Fisher grinned. "He does like money." He slapped the Harley's handlebars. "All right, man, I'll run it up the flagpole and we'll see who salutes."

Cassandra was sitting on my couch eating a peanut butter and jelly sandwich. The fact that she was eating was a good sign. "You know what you need in here? A TV."

I shook my head. "Nah."

"You don't have to hook up cable. Just a TV and a DVD player, like back at the safe house."

I smiled. "Did you miss the end of *The River Wild*? Turns out, the river did it."

Cassandra gave my arm a playful swat. "Hey, man! Spoilers!"

I sat down on the couch next to her. She smelled like cinnamon. "I'm glad you're feeling better."

Cassie smiled. "It's amazing what a good night's sleep can do."

Brave words from a brave woman. I knew it would take more than a good night's rest to recover from Johnny Rapoli.

Cassandra looked over at me. "I need a game."

"You feeling lucky?"

Cassandra stared directly at me. "We make our own luck. I believe hard work pays off. I believe in the odds. The numbers don't lie. You play the odds right enough times and eventually you win. It's as simple as that."

I didn't say, *If it's as simple as that, then why are you broke?* Instead, I said, "Hard work should pay off, but it doesn't always. There are billions of people all around the world who struggle. They work hard from sunrise to sundown, digging ditches, planting crops, taking care of children. Maybe they earn enough to eat, maybe not. Meanwhile, there other people straight-up lounging around in palaces made of gold. You think the folks in the palace work harder than the people in the field? Hell no."

Cassandra frowned. "What are you saying?"

"I'm saying the game is rigged. It's nice when hard work pays off, but it's not a given. Plenty of people work hard, get nothing, and then they die. Other people are born with everything and they die still clutching sacks of cash. That's just the way it is. The scales are crooked and always have been." I shrugged. "Maybe that'll change someday. I don't know."

Cassandra exhaled. "Goddamn, Jack, you're a real downer sometimes, you know?" She pulled a pack of cards from her purse and shook them into her palm. They flowed from her left hand to her right like a waterfall.

"I'm ready to play. I was born ready. You know me, Jack. I love the hustle. Those backroom games, man … it's like all of life boiled right down to its essence — risk, reward, danger — it's all right there."

I grinned. "Plus you like punishing those guys when they underestimate you. They call you 'baby' and 'darling' and then you flip the cards and take their shit."

Cassandra wrinkled her nose. "That's a nice bonus, but that's not what it's about. I want to be the best. Besides, what else would I do? Go back to school?"

"Sure. Why not? Nothing's written in stone. No one stamped *Professional Gambler* on your forehead when you were a baby. It's always possible to change your life."

Cassandra was silent for a minute. "Do you really believe that?"

"Yeah," I said. "I do."

CHAPTER 26

In my business, you make enemies. That's just the nature of the beast. If you're lucky, you know who your enemies are.

I wasn't sure about Freddy. Freddy was old school. He had been with The Old Man's organization until The Old Man bought the farm. That was nine years ago. Nowadays, the word was Freddy had retired. Now he was just a simple café owner, hanging out in his little social club on the Danforth, sipping espresso and watching soccer with his regulars. I didn't buy it for a second.

I took the subway over the Don Valley to Coxwell Station. Then I walked east along the Danforth to Freddy's bar. The place was tiny. Just six stools at the bar, three tables in the back, and one at the front. There were also three chairs outside on the sidewalk, pushed against the wall. That's where the smokers sat. The TV on the wall over the bar blared and the bottles glittered.

A man with a walrus moustache and a grey newsboy cap sat behind the bar near the front window, sipping espresso.

"Jack!" Freddy beamed and waddled out from behind the bar. He had always been big, but now he was obese. It suited him, though. It was hard to picture him any other way.

"Freddy."

We embraced.

He patted my back and beamed. "I haven't seen you since that thing with Tommy."

Tommy was gone and everybody knew it. At first there was talk that he had scraped together some cash and skipped town, heading off to Costa Rica or Aruba or someplace else where it wasn't winter six months of the year. But as the months went on and no one got any calls or postcards, people started to catch on to the fact that Tommy wasn't coming back.

"What do you hear?"

Freddy picked up his espresso from the bar. "Come with me." The man eased his bulk toward one of the tables at the back. He called over his shoulder, "You want a drink?"

"Yeah."

Freddy stomped behind the bar and poured us both a vodka. He handed mine to me and then went back to his perch.

Freddy and I drank. The TV was turned to Cable-Pulse 24. I used to sit and drink by myself in my old apartment and stare at this channel. There was always all kinds of info on the screen: traffic feeds, weather reports, stock tickers scrolling by. Life was happening all over the city, all at once.

"Y'know, Jack, I'm surprised to see you. I'm happy to see you, don't get me wrong, but I'm surprised."

"Oh yeah? Why's that?"

"After all that shit with Tommy, I figured you'd be cooling your heels in Costa Rica."

"I hear it's nice."

"Oh, it is. Waterfalls, flowers, monkeys … they got it all."

"That shit with Tommy was a long time ago."

"Thing is, Jack, Tommy disappearing was like throwing a pebble into a pond, you dig? That shit sends up ripples and those ripples keep rippling."

"Tommy made his own bed."

"No doubt, no doubt. Just between you, me, and the lamppost, the man was a real piece of shit."

I nodded.

"A made man goes missing, though … I figure the bosses got to do something."

"And you're saying that something is me."

Freddy nodded. "You were his bodyguard."

I shook my head. "No. I was paying off a debt."

"Either way, word is you saw the man last." Freddy shrugged. "Blame's got to fall somewhere." Freddy drained the last of his vodka. "There's a new guy on the council. He wants to clean house. They're sending a guy up from New York."

"You know what he looks like?"

Freddy smiled. "Yankees cap, *I Heart New York* T-shirt."

I smiled back. "Where'd you say he was from again?"

Freddy laughed. "See, that's why I like you, Jack. You tell most folks there's a hit man coming up from New York and they get all agitated. I tell you and you're sitting there joking around with a drink in your hand."

I shrugged. "Getting agitated isn't going to fix anything."

"No, sir, it certainly will not." Freddy pushed back from the bar and stood up. "So, you good? You need anything else?"

I sipped my vodka. "Tell you what. When the guy from New York shows up, shoot him in the head for me, will you?"

Freddy laughed and pointed at me. "You're a joker, Jack. Watch your back now, you hear?"

"One other thing."

"What, that wasn't enough?"

"I'm looking for a game."

The man's eyebrows shot up. "Yeah? You and Eddie have a falling out?"

"It's not like that. I've got a friend, a poker player. She's looking for a big game. I know the Canada Day Game is coming up. She wants in."

Freddy nodded. "You're talking about Cassandra?"

"Yeah, that's right."

Freddy kept nodding. "Good player. One of the best. She has a lot of heart."

"She does. Her backers crapped out on her, though. She needs the buy-in."

"You can't float her?"

I shook my head. "What can I say, Freddy? Times are tough all over."

The huge man laughed. "All right, all right. As a favour to you, I'll back her play. She and I will split any profits sixty-forty. I get the sixty."

"Come on now, Freddy."

"That's fair, my friend. That's more than fair."

It was highway fucking robbery. But those were the terms and they weren't going to get better. "Yeah, all right."

We shook on it.

CHAPTER 27

The man from New York came around the corner without a care in the world. Grover stepped forward and hit the hit man in the face with the butt of his gun. The man reeled back. I put him in a sleeper hold and choked him out.

Grover got under the man's shoulder and I got under the other, and together we dragged him through the alley to Grover's waiting car.

"I still think we should've done it right here," Grover said. "This guy's gonna get blood all over everything."

"You got plastic in the trunk, right?" I supported the man's full weight as Grover popped the trunk.

"Yeah, but ..." Grover looked down at his white pants. "See? There's a drop right there. Now I've got to burn this suit."

"The whole thing? Or just the pants?" I heaved the man into the trunk. He was still breathing. Good.

"Without pants, it's not a suit. I'm not Donald Duck, Jack. I'm not going to run around the city wearing a sailor hat and a jacket with no pants." Grover slammed the trunk closed.

We drove the guy to the boat. We tried to make it look like Mr. New York was drunk. Just three buddies out on a tear, wobbling down the dock for a midnight ride.

Right before we boarded the boat, Grover glanced over at me. "The guys who tipped me off … they're going to want something in return."

I nodded. Mr. New York was slipping. "Yeah, I figured. Come on, let's get him on board."

We chugged out toward the middle of the lake. The city lights twinkled in the distance.

Mr. New York was duct-taped to a chair in the cabin. Grover poured us some Scotch and then we settled in to wait for the man to wake up.

It didn't take long. Halfway through our second drink the man stirred and started straining at the tape. Grover set down his Scotch and winked at me. Then he walked over to the man taped to the chair. Grover slapped the man, hard.

The man stared at Grover with full-on contempt. Grover smiled at him, reached down, and snapped one of the man's fingers. The man screamed. Grover broke another finger. The man kept screaming.

"Stop."

Grover looked up at me with a frown on his face. "This guy tried to kill you, Jack."

I stared at the man. What had happened in his life to lead up to this moment?

"Someone sent you to kill me." I shrugged. "It didn't work out. Sometimes these things happen. You want a drink?" I took out my knife and started cutting the man's hands free.

Grover frowned. "What the hell, Jack?"

"Everyone gets a last meal, right?"

The man spit right in my face.

Grover fired twice. The man crumpled and slumped forward. I cut his arms and legs free and manoeuvred him onto the white canvas drop cloth. Grover set his gun on the table and knelt down. Together we started folding the canvas over the body.

"Get his legs, will you?"

We lugged the would-be hit man out of the cabin and over the railing. Grover tossed the man's gun in after him. There was a splash and then the lake swallowed him up.

We walked back into the cabin and sat there in the dark. Grover poured another Scotch. The waves rocked us slowly from side to side. We sat in silence for a minute.

"I'm thinking of making a change."

Grover glanced toward me. "Is that right?"

"Yeah. We live right on the edge of the fucking knife, all the goddamn time." I glanced out the cabin window. "You retired once. It was nice, right?"

Grover nodded. "Yeah, it was, at first. Then just lying on the beach started making me itchy, and I'm not talking about sand fleas."

"And now you're back."

"Now I'm back."

I paused. "Do you ever worry?"

Grover frowned. "What do you mean?"

"You ever worry that someone's going to sneak up behind you one day?"

Grover grinned. "They can try."

CHAPTER 28

In war, one side tries to demonize the other. They claim the other side isn't even human. Because if you saw the other side as fully human, with hopes and fears and loves and dreams just like you and the people you love, then it would be too damn hard to kill them. For most people, that is.

There's always some folks out there who enjoy killing. Maybe Mr. New York was one of them. The man was going to kill me and now he wouldn't. He was gone, but I was still here. I closed my eyes and I saw his face. His eyes widening as Grover raised the gun.

I opened my eyes, reached for the bottle, and poured four fingers of bourbon into a glass. I drank it in one long pull.

I had gone straight from the boat to Melody's house. When I walked into the living room, everything looked so normal. The books on the shelves, the photos on the wall. I leaned closer to one of the photos: Melody laughing with her friends outside a bar, the streetlight casting a halo behind them, snow coming down.

I heard the water running in the shower. Then the water turned off. "Hey, Jack, come in here a minute, would you?"

I walked down the hall and opened the bathroom door. A blast of steam escaped into the hallway.

Melody stepped naked from the shower. My eyes got wide. Her blond hair was darker now, slicked back against her head. Drops of water were rolling down the curves of her breasts. "Hand me that towel, would you, Jack?" I reached out and cupped her breasts. She smiled. I pinched her right nipple and she playfully swatted my hand away. The bathroom air was hot and steamy. I tried to reach my hand between her legs but she took a step back, then looked up at me and winked.

Melody moved past me and sashayed down the hall toward the bedroom. I followed, hypnotized by her fantastic ass. She climbed onto the bed and then turned to face me. She smiled, spreading her legs. "Lick me, Jack."

I walked over, knelt down, and spread her legs wider. I buried my face between her thighs. She tasted sweet like honey. Melody moaned and ran her fingers through my hair. She broke away and smiled. I reached for her, caressed her skin, and then grabbed her hips. She gasped as I flipped her onto her stomach. My fingers dipped into her folds. She moaned again and raised her ass toward me. I had a full rear view of her beautiful shaved pussy. I yanked down my pants. I was throbbing, jutting out like a cannon about to fire. I got behind her and pulled her closer. I slipped inside her warm slickness and began to move, slowly at first and then harder and faster. We rocked together. She moaned and I held her tight as we came, our bodies shuddering together.

Melody was quiet for a minute. We sat up and snuggled in together. She twirled her fingers through my chest hair.

"Jack, have you ever been in love?"

"Yes." I thought about Cassandra. I thought about Suzanne. "Have you?"

Melody grinned. Her long fake nails raked across my chest. "What's it like?"

CHAPTER 29

Melody and I were having fun together, but we weren't exclusive. I'd been down that road before and it never ended well. My last girlfriend, Suzanne, had gotten shot because of me. She survived, but if the bullet had gone an inch to the left it would've been a different story. I met women sometimes, mostly at bars, women who smiled at me with a certain light in their eyes. I could offer them a fun night or two, but nothing more than that. I didn't want to put anyone in harm's way ever again.

I took a shower, got dressed, said goodbye to Melody, and took the Queen streetcar back toward Chinatown.

Cassandra woke up and bolted upright when I came through the door. She scrambled for the knife sitting on the floor next to the couch.

"Whoa, whoa! It's only me."

She pressed her hand to her chest. "You scared the shit out of me."

I tilted my chin at the knife on the floor. "You take that from my desk?"

"Yeah. Hope you don't mind." Cassandra smiled her sad little half smile. "It makes me feel a little safer."

I walked over to my desk and made a beeline for the bourbon bottle. Cassie frowned. "You ever think about quitting drinking?"

The brown booze glugged into the glass. That sharp, rotted fruit smell. "Sometimes," I grinned, "when I'm hungover."

"I'm serious. The way you drink … you're killing yourself. You know how Jack Kerouac died?"

I shook my head.

"His guts blew up. An abdominal hemorrhage caused by too much drinking. He literally died drowning in his own blood."

I stared at the bourbon glass in my hand.

"I know some people in the Program. I could make some calls."

I set the bourbon glass down. "No. Don't worry about me."

"I do." Cassie stared into my eyes. "I don't want you to die."

"I'm alive right now and so are you." I picked up the glass of bourbon and knocked it back. "You got everything you need? Towels? Toothbrush?"

"Where are you going?"

"I'm heading down to the casino. Try to get some sleep, okay?"

"I'm serious, Jack. I don't want you to die."

I smiled. "That makes two of us."

CHAPTER 30

Eddie inhaled, exhaled. A thin curl of smoke hung briefly in the air and then vanished. "Bad news, Jack. Aunt Cecilia died."

I always thought Aunt Cecilia was going to live forever. She'd gone to sleep the night before in her Richmond Hill mansion, surrounded by gold-coloured furniture and goldfish and family photos in gold frames and all her other golden shit, and she never woke up. Vin found her in her bedroom, half on the floor, tangled in the sheets. He tried to revive her, but it was a no go. The entire time Vin was there, Aunt Cecilia's cellphone kept buzzing on the night table. Word would spread fast that she was gone.

I walked over Eddie's office rug to put my hand on the big man's shoulder. "I'm so sorry, Eddie."

Eddie exhaled. "It's fucked up, you know? I just saw her the other night."

"They're sure it was her heart?"

Eddie nodded. "That's the word. I've got my guys at the police station looking into it." Eddie's eyes narrowed. "I'll tell you what, though. If it wasn't her heart — if this shit comes back as murder — then a whole lot of motherfuckers are in for a world of hurt."

I nodded. "Just say the word."

Eddie patted his pockets, searching for his cigarettes. "Funeral's in three days. She wanted you to be a pallbearer."

"I'm honoured." I paused. "Why me, though? I thought she hated me."

Eddie smiled. "Are you crazy? She loved you, man. You know what she called you? *Ngo ge gwaijai.*"

"What's that mean?"

Eddie laughed. "Basically it means 'my white boy.' I'm telling you, man, she loved you. You saved Dawn's life. You think she'd ever forget?"

That was almost twenty years ago. Eddie was just getting started in the casino game. A gangster named King Diamond had decided to muscle in. To improve his bargaining power, King Diamond kidnapped Eddie's daughter. We got her back. And King Diamond? Let's just say that no one will ever see him again.

There was a knock on Eddie's office door. "Come in," he barked. Eddie's guy Josh popped his head through the door. "Sorry for interrupting, Boss. There's a guy upstairs looking for Jack."

Eddie raised an eyebrow. "Who is it?"

"Said his name was Kevin Rhodes."

Eddie and I looked at each other blankly. "You know a Kevin Rhodes?" he asked me.

I shook my head and turned to Josh. "What's he look like?"

Josh shrugged. "You know those guys down in Florida with speedboats full of cocaine? He looks like that."

Eddie and I went upstairs. The man I saw kicking back at the table near the front window of Eddie's restaurant was about thirty-something, with wavy light-brown hair and a sunburned face. One thick arm was thrown across the chair next to him. The top few buttons on his light-blue shirt were undone, revealing a gold chain glittering within a mat of chest hair so thick it looked like a pelt. The man grinned and stood up.

"Jack Palace? I'm Kevin Rhodes." He shook my hand and handed me a business card. "We had a mutual friend. He called himself The Chief." Rhodes smiled. "I was his lawyer."

I frowned. "What do you want?"

Rhodes kept smiling. "You got it backwards. It's not what I want, it's what I can do for you. You see, here in Ontario, after a person has been missing for at least seven years, they can be declared legally dead. Exceptions can be made if the individual has disappeared 'in circumstances of peril.' Like if a depressed person vanishes but a suicide note is found next to the lake, stuff like that."

I stared at the lawyer. "The Chief didn't leave a note."

"Oh, I know. But it's been" — Kevin Rhodes squinted at his notes — "nine years." The lawyer looked up and grinned. "I'm a little late. You're a hard man to find, Mr. Palace."

He slid an envelope across the table. *Ricin ... anthrax ... Unabomber-style letter bomb.*

"Sign here, will ya?"

"What is this?"

Rhodes grinned. "It's the deed to The Chief's trailer. Congrats, Mr. Palace. It's all yours."

CHAPTER 31

Gravel crunched under the tires as I drove up the long, curved driveway to The Chief's trailer. The big barn with the gym inside sat about fifty feet behind it. In the winter, we'd move from the trailer to the gym and then back again, tromping our boots down into the snow to make a path. The snow on top of the path would ice over and then our boots would crunch through the ice.

I left a lot of sweat on that barn floor — sweat and more than a little bit of blood. The Chief broke my arm once during a training exercise. I thought I had the drop on him, but I didn't. In my head, my arm made a sound like a twig snapping when The Chief broke it. Really there had been no sound, just a sudden lightning bolt of pain.

I got out of the car and walked through the weeds toward the trailer. One of the windows was broken and another one was boarded up. The roof was bent and swaybacked like a broken-down mule. The whole place was a lot smaller than I remembered. The Chief had filled this place with his spirit. When he lived here, the trailer and the barn buzzed with energy and activity. Even in quiet moments, sitting on the porch sharpening our knives, listening to the mooing of distant cows, hearing the rumble of trucks out on the highway. With him gone, the trailer had shrunk and started to collapse in on itself. Without The Chief, it was just an empty box.

I stood in front of the trailer door and pulled out the key the lawyer had given me. But I didn't open it. Instead I put the key back in my pocket and headed over to the barn.

The barn door opened with a creak. Shafts of sunlight were filtering through the cracks between the boards. The heavy bag was there, just as I remembered it. A little more rust on the chain and a little more duct tape on the bag, but other than that it was the same. The Chief had kicked my ass up and down this whole barn, but in the end, I learned.

I turned and walked back to the trailer. Once again, I stared at the front door. I didn't want to go in there and see The Chief's old stuff. His old blue couch, sagging in the middle; the tiny TV sitting on the TV stand he built himself; the papers and letters and books and bottles. The lemon-shaped soap dish sitting next to the kitchen sink. His clothes lined up and hanging in the closet. The remains of his life left behind, like a snakeskin after the snake moves on.

There were places and people I could call. Junk removal folks, estate sale folks. Not that The Chief had any antique spoons or anything like that. There were weapons stashed in the trailer and in the barn and all over the perimeter. There might be a bit of money stashed somewhere, too. Banded bills rolled up and tucked inside old mason jars and buried next to rocks and trees. Not a lot, just enough cash to help The Chief sleep at night. Some of the old tripwires might still be up in the woods, too.

I wasn't going to call anyone.

I went back to the car and popped the trunk. I pulled out a bottle of Jameson and walked back to the porch. I sat down on the white plastic chair and looked down to see The Chief's old ashtray on the weathered grey boards of the deck. The ashtray was still full, a heap of soggy rotten cigarette butts. I could almost see The Chief's nicotine-yellowed fingers rolling another smoke with his Zig-Zags and his Drum tobacco. I could hear his gravelly voice: "Well, Jack — whatcha gonna do?"

The wind whipped the grass. I opened up the bottle of Jameson and took a long pull. I sat there with the key in my hand and I drank.

I woke up in the morning and groaned. My back was stiff from sleeping on The Chief's porch. No — it was my porch now. I sat there on the porch for a minute listening to the birds. Then I stood up and drove back to the city.

CHAPTER 32

The casino was a hive of activity as people made preparations for Aunt Cecilia's funeral. Eddie came out of his office, followed by Vin. I blinked. Their heads were completely shaved. "For the funeral," Eddie said.

"Should I do that?"

Eddie smiled. "That's sweet, Jack. But no."

I slapped the car keys into Eddie's hand. We stood looking at each other for a minute, then Eddie adjusted his tie. "All right," he said, "here we go."

We drove out to a church in Scarborough. It was all dark wood and flowers. There was a man in the crowd with a too-small suit and a white walrus moustache. I knew who he was: Charlie the Vice Cop who had been trying to bust Cecilia for years. *Looks like the reaper beat you to it*, I thought.

The pallbearers lined up. We left the church and helped carry the coffin to the gravesite, then stood there in our dark suits with our hands folded respectfully.

At the gravesite, the minister said a few words. He said Aunt Cecilia was in a better place. Maybe it was true. There was no way to know. It's not like Aunt Cecilia was going to come back and tell us about it. The dead only come back in dreams.

I didn't go to my mother's funeral. Would I have gotten closure, seeing a shovelful of dirt hit the coffin? Most of the funerals I've been to, they don't start throwing dirt until all the mourners make their way back to the church or the funeral home for cookies and coffee and little sandwiches with the crusts cut off. And then it's the gravedigger's time to shine.

Closure. What's closure? That shit was for the movies. Get everything all wrapped up in a nice little package. In real life, trauma doesn't work like that. Trauma changes you forever. You can survive, you can even thrive, but you're different now. Seeing my mother get buried wouldn't have changed a goddamn thing.

I didn't even know she was dead until three months after the funeral. Some collections agency tracked me down, trying to get me to cough up the cash to pay her bills. I told them to get fucked. How many goddamn times had we moved in the middle of the night as she tried to skip out on her bills? All our money went to booze. Or our cash was hoovered up by yet another shiftless asshole who was pretending to give a shit about us — all those faceless "uncles." I split that scene when I was seventeen and I never looked back.

Back at the church, I stuffed a tuna sandwich into my mouth and headed for the door. On my way out, Eddie shook my hand. "Thanks for everything, Jack."

"She was a good woman, Eddie." Aunt Cecilia had been a vicious mobster, but that's not the kind of shit you say at a funeral.

"Where you headed?"

"There's something I gotta do." I frowned. "Can't put it off any longer."

I met Melody at her house. She was bustling around in the kitchen, slicing tomatoes, spreading mayo. "You want a sandwich?"

"I ate at the funeral."

"You sure? You know I'm famous for my club sandwiches." Melody smiled. "The secret is mayo. Lots of mayo."

She put her sandwich on a plate and carried it into the dining room. She sat down.

I remained standing. "It was you."

Melody looked over at me, her mouth full of club sandwich. "What?"

"You and Marcus, you boosted your dad's coke."

"Come on, man. That's crazy talk."

"You and Marcus went to your dad's house, ripped up his basement, and stole his cocaine."

Melody frowned. "It sounds so bad when you say it like that."

"How would you say it?"

"I was doing dear old Dad a favour. Bringing back Satan's Blood? He was going to get killed behind that shit. Yeah, I took the coke. No coke, no money, no Satan's Blood."

"Your dad could've been killed."

"You think I'm a fucking idiot? My dad was so drunk he could barely stand." Melody put her hands on the table. "Think about it, Jack. This could work out well for you, too. We sell that coke, we raise some cash. You take some of that cash — a loan, you understand — and you pay off Anton. He goes away happy. Cassandra's happy, which makes you happy. You pay me back and I'm happy." Melody's fingertips drummed against the table. "You see? Everybody's happy."

"Except Fisher and your dad."

"They get to live, man. They don't have to go to war with the Angels over a fucking pipe dream. So what do you say? You in?"

CHAPTER 33

Cowboy sat in the driver's seat of his Escalade with the AC blasting. Icicles were practically forming on the roof. I rubbed my arms. "You smuggling penguins, Cowboy? Got 'em locked in the trunk or something?"

Cowboy leaned forward and turned down the AC. "I like the cold. Keeps me sharp. This time of year it gets too hot, man, I can't even think. I'm like a robot winding down." Cowboy made a dying electronics sound and swung his arms around, pantomiming a robot losing power. Then he looked at me and winked.

"The math checks out. Four kilos isn't all that much in the grand scheme of things, but folks have had their heads chopped off for less. And we're talking four kilos of uncut. Once that shit's been stepped on, it's gonna be eight kilos at least. A key of uncut will run you about twenty-five grand if you're buying in bulk. Each gram can be sold for about a hundred bucks. See what I'm saying? Sell that shit by the rock and the price doubles. Twenty bones for a tenth of a gram means now each gram is worth two hundred bucks. A thousand grams in a kilogram … so at street level, if you're selling by the rock, your twenty-five-thousand-dollar kilo now is worth two hundred thousand dollars. But don't forget, that original key's been doubled because you've stepped on it with lactose and creatine and who the fuck knows what else. Some people use levamisole. You know what that shit is? It's used to deworm cattle. *Mmm-mmm*, delicious. Point is, doubled-up, your original kilo that cost twenty-five grand is now two kilos of crack worth four hundred thousand dollars on the street. The original four kilos that cost a hundred grand total are now eight kilos of crack worth one million, six hundred thousand dollars."

I blinked. "Goddamn."

Cowboy nodded. "That's a nice profit margin right there." He slapped the steering wheel. "Thanks for coming to me with this, Jack. Reminds me of the good ol' days."

The math checked out. I closed my eyes and I could smell Melody, that coconut and sunshine smell. "How much would you pay for the four kilos?"

Cowboy shook his head. "You got it wrong, Jack. I don't fuck with that shit anymore."

"Right. You're in the music biz now."

"That's, like, you know, a hobby." Cowboy laughed. "Thanks again, Jack. Good luck." Cowboy held out his hand and I shook it.

"Goodbye, Cowboy." I climbed out of the Escalade and stood in the parking lot while he drove away.

Maybe the math checked out, but Melody's coke scheme was still insane. Melody and Marcus couldn't retail 1.6 million dollars worth of crack all by themselves. As Marcus said, they didn't have the customers. He was also right on the money when he said that moving that much product a rock at a time would take forever. And as much as I enjoyed Melody's company, I wasn't exactly relishing the prospect of playing the heavy in Melody's imaginary drug empire. Plus, as Whitney Houston said, crack is wack.

As I saw it, there were only a few possible solutions.

One: Melody had to come clean. Admit everything and give Walter back his coke. Maybe he'd sell the shit and get his violent biker gang back in business. Or maybe he'd get stomped to death in the process. Hallmark didn't make a card for any of that. "Sorry I ripped off your coke, Dad." Right next to the lilac-covered cards for Grandma's birthday. If Melody came clean, that would make for decades of awkward family get-togethers, glaring at each other over the bones of the Thanksgiving turkey. Worse, that might be the final nail in the coffin when it came to their relationship. I didn't know if Walter would disown his daughter for stealing his four keys of uncut cocaine, but people have stopped speaking to each other for less.

Solution Two: wholesale that shit. Cowboy wasn't the only game in town. Sell the coke quick and be done with it. Melody wouldn't be happy with the smaller payday, but it would be a lot safer than standing on the corner with a vial of crack in your fist.

That was the missing part of Cowboy's equation. There were other dealers out there who wouldn't be happy with some brand-new competition. In that scenario, Melody and Marcus's baseball bats wouldn't mean shit. Maybe the bats intimidated suburban dads looking to toot a few lines on a Saturday night, but there were dealers out there with full-on, honest-to-God machine guns who were more than willing to protect their turf.

I took a cab to Fisher's place and climbed up the crumbling porch steps. The red warning sign greeted me at the door: OXYGEN IN USE. I thought about Daisy wasting away upstairs.

When Fisher opened the door, his eyes were red and puffy. At first I thought he was high. Then he wiped his eyes with the back of his hand. "Not a good time, Jack."

"I've got a line on your missing coke. Walter didn't take it. He was ripped off."

"You working for him now?"

"No, I'm not working for him."

"You tell that sonofabitch to give me back my shit."

"I'm telling you, he doesn't have it."

"Then who does?"

"Someone who's interested in giving it back."

Fisher glared at me and then his face softened. He left the door open and walked over to his tree trunk coffee table and picked up a pack of smokes. He tapped one out and lit it up, then collapsed back onto his old yellow floral couch. "You want me to wholesale that shit myself? I don't have time for that shit. I'm going to be busy over the next few days." Fisher exhaled a thick cloud of smoke. "A few years back, when Daisy could still travel, we went down to Vegas for a cancer convention. It was for patients, you know, like one giant support group, but I went down there with her to keep her company." Fisher chuckled. "Not that she needed it. Sometimes you need to be with people who really get where you're coming from, you know? People that are going through the same shit you are. It didn't take her long at all to make friends. They all went off together, and that was great, you know, fine with me. I walked around the strip, I made a little money playing black-jack, I checked out a few shoe shows. You know why they call 'em shoe shows?" Fisher grinned. "'Cause that's all those gals end up wearing — up on stage naked as jaybirds except for those sparkly high-heeled shoes.

"Anyway, one night I weave and wander back to our room and stagger through the door and there's Daisy, right in the middle of her room with her friends, these two old gals and this real pale red-haired gal who was young, Jack, like in her twenties ... folks that young shouldn't get sick like that. Hell, no one should get sick like that. But anyway, these gals are sitting in the room with Daisy and I stomp on in and just stand there blinking and they all start laughing, this high-pitched laughter just rolling right over everything. Turns out they're all high as balls. They've been sharing their pain meds around and washing them down with good old-fashioned American bourbon. That pale red-haired gal was grinning like a cat, sitting all splayed out on an armchair by the window. The two old gals — turns out they were together, you know, a couple ... Doris and, uh, I can't remember the other one's name. Gail? Anyway, they're all lolled back in the bed and Daisy is in the other bed and the sliding glass doors to the balcony are open and the sound from The Strip is coming in, bass bumping from cars and one man just flat-out howling, bringing up some deep-down despair from inside his body, gone primal from drinking and losing money all day. I stumbled over and shut the door and these gals are still laughing, tears rolling down their cheeks."

Fisher ground out his cigarette. "That was the last time I can remember Daisy being happy." Fisher stared up at me. "She always wanted to go back, but I guess it ain't happening now. She's gone, Jack." Fisher looked away. "No more pain."

"I'm sorry, Fisher."

"I'm going to sell this place. Cash out of this whole damn city and go south. Or London, maybe, or Sault Ste. Marie. Maybe find a little gal somewhere to share my bed." Fisher chuckled. "I'm not too old to start a family. Big ol' backyard with a swing set and everything. I can stand out there grilling up some steaks while the sun goes down." Fisher nodded. "Sounds pretty sweet, doesn't it?"

"Yeah, it does."

We sat there in the dark while the clocks tick-tocked.

CHAPTER 34

I took the bus down Vaughan Road to St. Clair West station and then I hopped on the subway. There was a woman sitting a few seats away who was obviously in some kind of mental distress. She was rooting around inside her filthy sweater, catching tiny bugs and then smearing them on the seat next to her. I couldn't tell if the bugs were real or imaginary. If they were real, they were probably bedbugs. The shelters were riddled with them. I got up and walked off the subway at the next stop. I didn't get on the next subway car. I waited for an entirely different train. Bedbugs, man. The bug woman needed help, but I couldn't help her. You can't help everyone, but if you try, you can still help some.

I made it back to my office and sat down behind the desk. *I should go legit*, I thought. Clean the joint up, get a couple of landlines, maybe a brass nameplate for my desk and a sign for the door: PALACE SECURITY. That had a nice ring to it.

I poured myself some bourbon and then I poured my plant some water. "Palace Security. What do you think, plant?"

It was probably just a breeze, but the plant bobbed its leaves yes.

There was a knock at the door. I shuffled over and peered through the peephole. Eddie was alone, standing there in the hallway in his black suit and skinny tie. The peephole gave a fisheye effect, making him look like an album cover from the early '90s. I fumbled with the locks and swung open the door.

"There's a guy downstairs to see you, Jack. Says his name is Marcus."

I followed Eddie down the stairs. Marcus was pacing at the front of the restaurant. He was agitated as all hell.

"You were right, man. Someone trashed my apartment. They were looking for the shit, the coke. Gotta be."

A family of diners was giving us the eye. "Let's go upstairs," I suggested.

Inside my office, Marcus was noticeably calmer. He stopped pacing but was still tugging on his shirtsleeve.

"You want something to drink?" I asked.

"No, no. No thanks."

"Your place was trashed, huh? You think it was Fisher or Walter?"

"I don't know, man. It's not like they left a calling card."

"Do you have any security cameras?"

"No." Marcus shook his head. "Nothing like that." He shuddered. "If I had been there …" Marcus looked at me, his eyes wide. "Man, I gotta get out of here."

I nodded. "I know a place."

Marcus and I sat on the porch of The Chief's old trailer, kicking back on the crappy plastic chairs, watching the wind ripple through the fields. Three dark shadows were moving in slow lazy circles above us.

Marcus tilted his head back. "What kind of birds are those?"

"Turkey vultures."

Marcus looked worried.

I smiled. "Don't worry, they won't eat us. They're just checking us out, making sure we're not dead."

Marcus smiled. "Not dead yet." He leaned back and turned his face to the sun. "Man, it's nice out here. You live here?"

I shook my head. "I live in the city. But I've been thinking more and more about making a change." I squinted. "Maybe I'll open up my own security shop."

Marcus nodded. "I hear that. I got family in Halifax. I might move out there someday, buy my own place. Cheaper than Toronto, that's for sure."

I tilted my chin toward the trailer door. "You want a beer?"

"Nah, no thanks." Marcus smiled. "I quit drinking a few years back. Figured I drank up my lifetime supply. Back before I quit, I went to the doctor about these head-aches I was having and he ran all kinds of tests. My head was fine, but the tests flagged my liver. Doc said my liver was 'high functioning.' I thought, shit, sounds good to me. Like my liver was an honours student or something. But nah, turns out high functioning is bad, at least when it comes to livers. It was working overtime, struggling to flush out the toxins from all that booze I was guzzling." He shrugged. "I miss it sometimes. Drinking can be fun, you know? You go out, you see friends, you meet people, random shit happens. One minute you're sitting in the bar with a beer in your hand and then BAM! Next thing you know you're at some loft party and the music is bumping and there's a clown show going on with trapezes and shit, and then the girl sitting next to you whips off her top." Marcus chuckled. "That's what I miss the most, the randomness."

"Being on the run from drug-dealing bikers is pretty random."

Marcus looked down at the ground. "Yeah," he muttered.

I wanted to stand up, walk into the trailer, and grab an ice-cold beer from the fridge, but I didn't want to drink in front of Marcus. "How'd you meet Melody?"

Marcus smiled. "We went to high school together. We were lab partners in biology. We were dissecting rats and she made a cat's cradle out of the rat intestines. I thought that shit was hilarious. So out there, you know?" He grinned, remembering. "That's who she was back then — dyed black hair, black tights, black Doc Martens. She had a faded jean jacket with all kinds of buttons and shit on it. I remember she had one button that was a swastika with a red slash drawn across it. I thought that was kind of silly at the time. Like, *of course* you're against Nazis, who the fuck isn't against Nazis?"

Marcus got quiet for a minute. "These days, I don't know, man. Maybe I was naive. Shit, maybe I'm still naive." He glanced over at me. "I'm no coke kingpin, you know? I used to party a lot, back in the day. I do a few lines now and then, but nothing too serious. Some people, man, they do one line and BAM, that's it, now they're fiending for that shit forever. Me, I can take it or leave it. Melody …" Marcus ducked his head. "Well, let's just say I didn't flag it as a problem at the time. It was her idea to start dealing, but she didn't phrase it like that. The way she pitched it, it was all about saving money. The more you buy, the cheaper per gram it gets. We were used to buying a gram or two and blowing through it all in a night, but then we started buying eight balls and selling off a gram here and a gram there … then we'd take the profit and roll it over, turn it into more coke and do the whole thing again." Marcus nodded. "As long as you don't hoover up the profits yourself, you can start stacking cash pretty damn quick."

"Don't get high on your own supply."

"You got it." Marcus laughed. "Thing is, everybody does. At first, that was the whole point. We sold shit to bring down the cost of our own shit. Then Melody started getting ambitious, talking about how she could get more shit from some dude she knew at the club. At the time I just kind of laughed it off, you know. Like, 'Whatever, Melody. You're trippin'.' But then she showed up to my dorm room one day with a full ounce and I knew she was serious. Problem was, that ounce had been stepped on so many times it was like a marching band had trampled that shit." Marcus shrugged. "We bagged it up and sold it anyway. Then Melody started looking around for a new connect. I thought maybe she could ask her dad, you know? He was this badass biker, no doubt he had all kinds of connections. But Melody just looked at me like I was crazy. Apparently her dad was more on the muscle side, you know? He knew people who knew people, but Melody didn't want her dad to be all up in her business." Marcus grinned. "Sometimes there's Daddy-Daughter dealers, but that shit's pretty rare. Most parents, you know, even if they're dealing, they want to keep their kids far away from that shit. And likewise if the kid is dealing, they don't want their parents poking around and finding their stash in the closet underneath the comic books or whatever." Marcus shrugged. "Shit, I figured it was worth a try."

"Well … you're in it now."

"Yeah." Marcus watched the wind ripple through the grass. "I'm not a drug dealer, man. I was just selling shit to put myself through school. Melody, though … man, Melody's trying to get me to go to places I don't want to go."

"Did you help her steal Walter's coke?"

Marcus shook his head. "That was all her. She waited until her dad passed out and then she just walked off with the shit. Busted up a few commemorative plates and shit to make it look like a real robbery."

"Commemorative plates?"

"I don't know, man, collectables and shit. Walter's big into *Star Trek*."

"Then Melody tried to put the blame on Fisher."

Marcus nodded. "Yeah. Or me."

Marcus and I were quiet for a minute. Finally I cleared my throat. "You've been doing some thinking."

"Hell yeah, I've been thinking. Don't get me wrong, Melody's a fun person. Hell, you know that. Problem is, she's all about fun. Sooner or later, that shit's gonna catch up with her. What happens when the fun stops? She's not exactly the responsible type. No offence."

"I'm not offended."

"I mean, I know you guys are tight."

"It's like you said, we're just having fun."

We were quiet again. Farm machinery rumbled in the distance. A flock of birds flew by. "We never hooked up," Marcus said, "in case you were wondering."

"None of my business."

"She's not my type." Marcus squinted. "I don't think I have a type."

"Like I said. None of my business."

"We've been friends a long time. That's it."

"Friends and business partners."

"Yeah."

"And now you're having second thoughts."

Marcus chuckled, but there was no humour there. "Second thoughts, third thoughts, fourth thoughts." He looked at me. "I want out, Jack."

I looked over at Marcus. "Well," I said, "maybe I can help with that." I handed Marcus a shopping bag. "There's some cold cuts, bread, cheese, mustard. A couple of apples. I got the power turned on yesterday but it's a mess in there." I reached into the shopping bag and pulled out a box of garbage bags. "I've got cleaning supplies, too. Rubber gloves and shit. You help me get the place in shape and you can stay for as long as you want. There's no cable TV, but there are some books. Some magazines, too, but they're about nine years out of date."

"What's the Wi-Fi password?"

I just stared at him.

He looked down at his shoes. "Never mind," he muttered.

CHAPTER 35

I listened to classical music as I drove back to the city. I don't often listen to classical. All those screeching violins set my teeth on edge. Give me some nice Max Roach and Clifford Brown any day. This stuff was okay, though. It was gentle, quiet, and soothing. I spun the wheel and headed for the Starlight.

The club lights made everything look purple. Melody sashayed up to me in a white push-up bra and a lacy white thong. She spread a silk scarf over a bar stool and sat down next to me. Her mouth was smiling but her eyes were hard. "Where's Marcus?"

"He's safe."

"Yeah, but where —"

"Maybe better if you don't know." I signalled to the bartender and pointed to Melody. The bartender nodded and poured out a glass of pink champagne. This was a scam. The "champagne" was nothing but ginger ale and food colouring. *Champagne for my real friends; real pain for my sham friends.* I slipped the bartender a twenty. The cost of doing business.

Melody shook her head. The "champagne" bubbled in front of her, untouched. "That devious motherfucker. He's up to something, isn't he?"

"He's just trying to finish school in one piece."

Melody frowned. "What does that mean?"

"It means he's smart. He knows that someone — Fisher, your dad, maybe both — is going to come looking for that coke."

Melody laughed. "Oh Jesus, not this again."

"It's already happened. His place was trashed. Was it Walter?"

Melody shook her head. "My dad wouldn't do that."

"Fisher, then?"

Melody squinted. "How would Fisher know about Marcus?"

"Has Marcus ever come to meet you here?"

"Yeah."

"There you go. Fisher saw him here with you, followed him home, and tossed the joint. That means he suspects you might have the coke, too. Cut your losses, Mel. Accept the world for what it is. Wholesale the shit and be done with it."

"You're asking me to give up a million bucks."

"I'm asking you to give up a million bucks in imaginary pretend sparkly unicorn money and walk off into the sunset with actual real-life honest-to-goodness cold hard cash. Real money, Mel."

Melody wrinkled her nose. "I like it when you call me Mel. It's cute."

I stood up. "Think it over, okay? I'm going to be away for a few days."

"Yeah? Where you headed?"

"Up north. Georgian Bay."

Melody smirked. "A fishing trip?"

"No," I said. "Business."

CHAPTER 36

I carried the suitcase to the rental car. No sense piling more miles onto one of Eddie's vehicles. In the alley behind the casino, Cassandra smiled at me. "Did you make a mix tape?" I shook my head. She frowned. "How about snacks? Crackers? Granola bars? Club soda? C'mon, Jack. Haven't you ever been on a road trip before?"

"Club soda?" Most of my road trips involved a trunk full of gear — knives, ropes, night-vision goggles. I was hoping this trip would be a nice change of pace.

Cassie and I drove until the city sidewalks turned to fields. We stopped for lunch at a little café in Markdale, where we sat outside at a picnic table and ate egg salad sandwiches with tomato slices, dill pickles, and potato chips on the side. Everything was crisp, fresh, and delicious.

We kept driving. Cassandra played with the radio until she found some classic rock. She was wearing dark sunglasses with dark frames. Her hair was pulled back into a tight bun. She looked over at me and smiled. "Thanks for this, Jack."

"All I did was get you in. The rest is up to you."

Usually Freddy Johns hosted the Canada Day Game in a plush room at the Royal York Hotel. This year, though, the game had moved north. One of the guys from Hamilton, Silvio Esposito, had decamped to his private island in Georgian Bay for the summer and was too old and sick to come back to the city. As a favour, Freddy was bringing the game to him.

We made good time. We got up to Sauble Beach in three and a half hours. From there it was another hour to Silvio's island, but we would come back here for the night, put some distance between us and the poker players at Silvio's.

The car tires crunched on the white gravel of the parking lot as I pulled up in front of our rental cottage. Sauble Beach was about a ten-minute walk away. When I rented the place, I made sure there were at least two beds.

Inside, Cassie looked around and nodded. "Looks like a cottage, all right." She pointed to the bookshelf. "Look, they've got Clue."

I walked over and picked up the box. "The problem with these cottage games is they're always missing a piece or two." I opened up the box. It was completely empty. I blinked. Cassandra burst out laughing.

I walked back outside to get Cassie's bag from the trunk. My boots crunched in the gravel. The sun was going down. Suddenly, I froze. A man in a white suit was leaning against my car.

"Grover." It was strange seeing him outside of his usual context. I felt like a little kid who had just seen his teacher at the grocery store. As a kid, you think the teachers just live at the school. When you're not there, they just get frozen in cryogenic tubes or something. When that morning bell rings, the teachers are defrosted and the day begins.

"Howya doin', Jack?"

I frowned. "Did you follow me?"

"You weren't checking for tails." Grover shook his head. "Sloppy, Jack, sloppy. What would The Chief say?"

"What do you want?"

"I'm here for the fireworks." Grover held up a knife and grinned.

I shook my head. "You're crazy."

Grover looked hurt. "Mental health is no laughing matter, Jack. There's still a lot of stigma there."

"I didn't mean …"

Grover laughed. "Here, take this." He offered me the knife, hilt first. "Freddy's got to go. Do it during the fireworks, just in case he screams."

I grabbed the knife and tucked it into my jacket, just to get it out of sight. I stared at the little man. "What are you talking about? Freddy's helping me, Grover."

"Helping you into an open grave, maybe." Grover narrowed his eyes. "You really think he tipped you off about Mr. New York out of the goodness of his heart?"

In my head I heard the splash Mr. New York had made as his body hit the lake. Grover shook his head.

"That was a smokescreen. A ruse to make you let down your guard."

"You're way off base."

"Am I? Think about it. Now you trust him, right? You trust him enough to come on up to a gangster's private island."

A family of four crunched through the gravel on the way to their cabin. Grover turned on a brilliant smile. "Evening, folks. Beautiful tonight, isn't it?" He waited until the family passed by, then turned back to me and hissed, "What the fuck do you think is going to happen on that island? You go out there, you're not coming back."

"I'm going, Grover. Cassandra needs this."

"I thought you might say that."

"Grover … don't do anything stupid."

Grover grinned. "Who, me?" The little man looked around at the trees hanging over the cottage parking lot and breathed in deep. "Man, smell that fresh country air."

CHAPTER 37

Cassandra laughed, raking in a mountain of chips. There were five other guys at the table, most of them wearing track suits and gold chains: Gangster Casual. None of them looked happy.

Freddy sidled up to me. As host he'd gone more upscale, and was wearing a white shirt and a tie and suit pants that he must've had made special. They were about the size of a two-person tent. "Remember in the joint, playing for cigarettes?" Freddy chuckled. "Shit, I don't even smoke."

"Yeah." I didn't like to think about The Inside. I did my time, kept my head down, yet I still got jumped. I would've died if Tommy hadn't stepped in and made the attackers back off.

Silvio Esposito sat at the head of the table, an oxygen tank at his feet. I thought of the warning sign at Fisher's house. Silvio's chip stack was dwindling. He frowned, rubbery lips stretching across his toothless face. "C'mon! We playing cards, or what?"

Freddy grinned. "You heard the man. Ante up, gents. You too, Cassandra."

Everyone put in their ante. The dealer dealt the cards. Half the table folded right away. The flop came up and scared off one more. It came down to just two: a man named Ricky the Rabbit and Cassandra. Cassandra grinned and flicked her finger toward the centre of the table. "All in."

Ricky glared at her. His cards were face down in front of him. Slowly he peeled the cards up, took a look, then let them back down. He shuffled his chips, letting them clack together. Behind him one of Freddy's goons in an all-white track suit shifted his feet impatiently. Cassandra sat still like a statue. Her smile didn't waver. Her ruby-red lipstick was perfect. She was dressed to the nines in a slinky black dress. Her neckline was plunging. I stared over at the pale tops of her breasts and then forced myself to look away.

Ricky sneered. "Call."

Cassie flipped her cards. "Three aces."

Ricky the Rabbit stood up so fast he kicked over his chair. Instantly, two of Freddy's goons were at his side, latching on to his arms. Rabbit's long face was twisted up with fury. The veins were popping out on his neck. He struggled, but the goons held him tight. The Rabbit's eyes bulged. "Cheating bitch!"

Silvio held up a hand. Instantly the room fell silent. He took a hit of oxygen and struggled to get out of his overstuffed chair. His bodyguard, Dante, grabbed his hand and helped him up. "This woman ... is a guest ... in my home." Silvio stared at the Rabbit. "You're done." He gestured to the goons. "Get him out of here."

The goons glanced over at Freddy. Freddy nodded.

"Wait!" Ricky the Rabbit regained his composure. "Silvio, wait. I'm sorry."

The old man grimaced. "Fuck that. You disrespect a woman in my house?" Silvio jabbed his finger toward the door. Ricky the Rabbit hung his head as the goons took him by the arms and led him out.

The game continued. Cigars were lit and cards were flipped. The first round ended. Cassandra smiled behind her mountain of chips. Everyone stood up to stretch their legs.

"I'm up, Jack." Cassandra's eyes gleamed like marbles. A few strands of hair were plastered across her forehead.

"Time to walk away."

Cassandra shook her head. "That's not how it works. We play until someone rakes in all the chips." She smiled. "Winner take all."

She turned her back to me and headed back to the game.

I felt sick. I walked over to the sideboard and poured myself a Scotch.

Freddy Johns stepped up to me. "Gettin' smoky in here. How about you and I take a walk?"

Outside, the crickets were chirping.

Freddy looked up at the sky. "Nice night."

"So far, so good."

"It's nice to see the stars." He flicked the butt of his cigar into the gravel. "You don't see the stars in the city." Freddy squinted at me. "This thing with Tommy … it's got to end." I kept quiet, but Freddy kept talking. "I've been talking to the bosses. I'm real close to working it out."

"What do you need from me?"

"See, here's where it gets tricky." Freddy gazed out at the lake. Moonlight rippled on the surface of the water. "We need a name."

"You need a fall guy."

"Yeah, a patsy. Except in this case, I'm pretty sure this guy was actually there."

I stared at Freddy. "You know I can't throw anyone under the bus."

"No, no, of course not. I would never ask you to do anything like that."

"Why are you helping me, Freddy?"

"Who's the guy?"

"Sammy DiAngelo. You know him?"

"Can't say that I do."

"He fucking hates your guts, Jack. But I'm talking to some of the others on the council. It's looking good. DiAngelo's a solid soldier — he'll do what he's told. I go back to them with a name, you'll stop getting visitors from New York. You catch my drift?"

"You said you're looking for one name in particular."

"Yeah. This guy's been a real thorn in our side for years. One day he's helping us, another day he's knocking over our counting houses and robbing us blind." Freddy squinted. "You know who I'm talking about. I just need to hear you say it."

"I appreciate you going to bat for me. But you know I can't give you a name."

"This would be good for all of us, Jack."

I didn't say anything. Freddy sighed. "All right, if that's the way it's got to be, we'll figure out another way."

"I owe you one, Freddy."

"Yeah." The big man grinned. "You do."

CHAPTER 38

The game dragged on and on and on. Cards, cigars, Scotch, sandwiches. I was bored as shit. It was one thing to play poker, something else to be stuck on the sidelines. I kept glancing at the windows and the darkness beyond, expecting Grover to come popping up with a machine gun at any minute. He didn't. The cards flipped. Cassandra raked in another pot. At 1:47 in the morning, it was down to her and Silvio. I had to give the old man credit. He had really hung in there.

Silvio scowled at Cassandra over his mountain of chips. "All in."

Cassandra sat blank-faced for several seconds. Then she glanced up at Silvio and smiled. "Call."

Everyone in the room leaned in. I noticed Freddy was standing, gripping the arm of one of Silvio's antique chairs. The dealer's face was impassive, like one of those giant stone heads from Easter Island. He flipped over the final card.

Silvio turned over his cards. "Full house."

Cassandra stayed still like a statue. She flipped her cards. She had made an ace-high straight, but it wasn't good enough. She stood up and held out her hand to Silvio. "Congratulations."

Cheers went up. Freddy blanched like a rattlesnake had just bit him on the dick, but then he recovered, grinned, and patted Silvio on the back. The old man cackled.

I blinked. It was all over.

The wind rustled the trees as we walked back to the dock. Little waves were lapping against the rocks. Cassandra didn't look at me. "I was winning, Jack, right up till the end."

"Yeah," I said. "Sometimes that happens."

Back on the mainland, Cassie and I climbed back into the rental car. It smelled like plastic. I turned on the radio because the silence was stifling.

"I'm sorry, Jack."

"Yeah," I said. "Me, too."

The engine hummed, the tires bumped along the road, and Cassandra stared out the window at the darkness beyond. "Maybe it's a sign," she said. "Maybe it's time to hang it all up. Go back to school, become a teacher."

"You'd be a great teacher."

Cassandra smiled. "I'd be a shitty teacher. Are you kidding? All those snot-nosed brats and their overprotective parents. 'Why didn't Little Johnny get an A?' 'Because your Johnny is a lazy fucking idiot who didn't do any goddamn work, that's why.'"

We drove in silence the rest of the way. Darkness, headlights, grass, and trees. I saw a deer standing by the side of the road, eyes glowing in the headlights. I slowed down and gave the horn a honk. The deer bounded off, back into the woods.

Back at our cottage, everything was just as we had left it. The Clue box still sat empty on the table. Cassandra watched me look for Grover. All the rooms were empty. "Everything okay? No bogeymen?"

"Not tonight."

We stood there awkwardly, facing each other. "Well," she said, "good night." She went into the bedroom and shut the door. I poured myself a Scotch and sat on the couch, the lamp beside me glowing in the dark.

In the morning she was gone. This time she left a note:

Dear Jack: thanks for everything. I've gone back to the city to rustle up some cash. I'm going to dig myself out of this hole one chip at a time. Sorry I took the car. Rent another one and I'll pay you back, one of these days. Thanks again. Cassandra.

I made myself a coffee and drank it on the porch. Families walked past, heading for the beach.

"Jack." I whipped my head around and there was Grover. The little man stood by the side of the cottage. I blinked. He was wearing a pair of white shorts and a T-shirt with a picture of a giant grinning mosquito on it. Above the mosquito it said, *I Gave Blood on the Bruce*. That was where we were, the Bruce Peninsula. I had never seen Grover wearing shorts before.

"Morning," I said. "You want a coffee?"

"Yeah, sure."

We sat on the porch and drank our coffees. Grover squinted up at the sun. "Gonna be a hot one."

I looked over at him. "Do you want to know how last night went? Or do you already know?"

"I saw Cassandra leave early this morning. She didn't look too happy."

"You were watching us."

Grover nodded. "Trying to keep you safe, old man."

I tilted my head. "You're older than me, aren't you?"

"Point is, you're up here in Cottage Country but you're still surrounded by gangsters. You talk to Freddy last night?"

"Yeah," I said, "I did." I was quiet for a minute. I sipped my coffee. The caffeine was zinging through my bloodstream. The bitter taste lingered on my tongue. "They're gunning for you, Grover."

"Yeah," he said, "I know." He laughed. "You and me both. At least we're in good company, right?"

A man walked by carrying an oversized beach bag, an inflatable air mattress shaped like a giant piece of pizza, and a little blond boy who was probably about four years old. The Rolling Stones song "Beast of Burden" went through my head. The man trudged on, heading for the lake.

Grover put down his cup. "You want to head back together? We could get some ice cream and stop to see the sights. Got to be a World's Biggest Ball of Twine around here somewhere."

I didn't want to go back. At least not yet. I smiled at Grover. "Fuck that," I said. "I'm going to the beach."

CHAPTER 39

They never put on sunscreen in action movies. "I gotta stop that runaway train, but first let me put on some sunscreen." Even in a lot of beach movies, they never put on sunscreen. The needs of the body are an inconvenient reality. Kind of like how you never see the toilets on the Starship Enterprise.

It was the day after Canada Day. A lot of people had already left to go back to the city, but Sauble Beach was still full of happy families. One family was swimming in their turbans, laughing in the waves. Two teen girls in bikinis were posing by the water's edge while another girl snapped their picture. Memories.

I didn't want to think about anything. I wanted to lie on the beach and do nothing at all. Last night's booze was working its way out of my system. I chugged water from my plastic water bottle. There was sand stuck to the outside of the plastic so the bottle was gritty in my hand. The combination of the water and the sun was burning away my hangover.

A blond woman in official-looking clothes was striding along the beach, coming this way. I figured she was a park ranger or something. I had noticed her earlier when she'd been walking the other way. She wasn't wearing a hat and her skin was flushed pink from the sun. She smiled at me. "Hi, how are you?"

I nodded and smiled back. "You're not wearing a hat. It's pretty sunny out here."

"Yeah. I was wearing one yesterday, but, you know, it gets pretty hot. Were you here yesterday?"

I shook my head. "Nope."

"It was pretty crazy."

"Yeah, I bet. Were you giving lots of tickets?"

She nodded. "For barbecues. And parking. People were parking their cars on private property."

I thought about the little church I had passed on the way here, with its empty parking lot and NO PARKING sign. It didn't seem very Christian to me, but then again, what did I know? I never went to Sunday school.

I smiled. "You must hate long weekends, huh?"

The waves crashed. The sun framed her face perfectly. "I wouldn't say *hate*. Dislike, yeah. At some point the extra money won't be worth it." She smiled back at me. "I'll just call in sick."

"What's your name?"

"Molly."

"Nice to meet you, Molly. My name's Jack."

The cautious, paranoid little fucker that lived deep inside my brain was setting off alarm bells, trying to get my attention. *She's a cop, Jack! What the hell, man?* But no, she wasn't a cop, not really. She was a bylaw officer, busting illicit barbecues and off-leash dogs.

I tilted my head back toward the dunes. On the other side was the street and across the street was a bar. A line of motorcycles was parked out front, gleaming in the sun. "You ever go to that bar over there?"

She nodded. "Yeah, sometimes. There's a cover band that plays there that's pretty good. They're actually playing tonight."

"Oh yeah?" I downed the last sip from my water bottle. "Maybe I'll see you there."

She smiled. "Yeah. Maybe you will."

The band sucked. I thought maybe they'd get better if I had a few more beers, so I had a few more. Then Molly walked in. She said hi to a woman sitting at the bar and ordered a beer. Then she saw me and her face lit up. She headed over, looking all cute in her civilian clothes. She wore a white tank top and cut-off jean shorts that really hugged the curves of her fantastic ass. She grinned, tilting her chin toward the band. "What did I tell you? Pretty good, right?"

I smiled back. "They suck."

Molly blinked. Then she laughed. "You're honest. I like that." She looked at me closely. "Tell me something, Jack. Are you married?"

"Nope."

"Seeing anyone?"

"Yes. But we're not exclusive."

"Does she know that?"

I smiled. "She does." I stood up. "I'm going to get another beer. You want anything?"

Molly was looking right into my eyes. Without breaking eye contact, she raised her full bottle of beer to her lips and chugged it all. She smiled. "Yeah, I'll have another beer, too."

We fell through the door of Molly's place, kissing, grabbing, hungry for each other. She tugged off my T-shirt. I yanked down her pants. In seconds we were both naked. We kissed, our bodies rubbing together. She took me by the hand and led me to the bedroom.

Once we got inside, I threw her on the bed. She squealed.

"Get on all fours."

Her face was flushed, a few blond hairs stuck to her sweaty cheeks. She got down on all fours and raised that fabulous ass to me.

I pulled her closer and slipped two fingers into her pussy. She was wet and ready. I rolled on a condom and pushed inside. She gasped. I pushed in again, slow and steady. She was making little mewling sounds, like a cat. "Oh God … Jack … Jack…"

She shook when she came. I grabbed her hips and pulled her close as I came, too. I felt like a rocket exploding, my body enveloped in white light.

Afterward, we lay back, sweating on the tangled sheets. The big blond snuggled up to me. "What are you thinking about?"

"Justice."

She smiled. "Something tells me you're not talking about barbecues on the beach." She traced her finger along the scars on my chest. "Were you in the army?"

I nodded, slowly. "Something like that." I rolled over. "What's your number? I'll give you a call."

She smiled and shook her head. "You don't have to do that. It was a fun night. Maybe we should leave it there."

Alone, I walked back along the beach. Two gulls fought over a french fry. I didn't want to go back to the city. I wanted it to be summer forever. But that wasn't going to happen. In a few months, all those big Sauble waves would be frozen solid. Jagged peaks of snow-covered ice rising from the lake like dragon's teeth. And I would be back in the city, back to the sirens and the smog.

For now, the sun was shining and the waves were breaking and the lake smelled just like a lake should. I closed my eyes and breathed in deep.

CHAPTER 40

Back to the city. Back to Cassandra.

Cassandra, Cassandra.

When we were first dating, her name was like a waterfall. I'm no poet, but when you're in love, everything is poetry. Splashed with mud by a bus rushing by in the rain? Poetry. Bird shits on your head while you're sitting on a bench? Poetry. Punched in the nuts by some deadbeat you're trying to shake down for the money he owes? That shit is pure poetry. Okay, maybe not the nuts thing. But when you're in love, at the beginning, every single moment you're with your honey is like a scene in the goofiest, most ridiculous rom-com you've ever seen. Thing is, too many people get Real Life confused with the movies. Those rom-coms aren't documentaries. People like happy endings. The problem is, Real Life doesn't always work like that.

Did I still love Cassandra? Of course I did, on some level. Time had changed her and it had changed me, too. You can't step in the same river twice. Ain't no fool like an old fool. You can't teach an old dog new tricks. I sipped my Scotch, and then I had another sip. I looked over at my plant sitting on my desk and said, "Cheers." The booze was filling me with a warm nostalgic glow. When I looked at Cassandra now, I saw a different woman than the woman I had loved.

Cassandra and I, that was a long time ago. Some days it seemed like yesterday, other days it seemed like a million years ago. Prehistoric fossil memories decaying into carbon. Forgotten photos on a thrift shop shelf. *Forget about it, Jack. Let the past be the past.*

Still, though, I couldn't help but imagine. What if? What if we got back together? What if I stepped out of the shadows and went straight? Palace Security. We could move to the suburbs, have a bunch of kids. I could be out there mowing the lawn every second Saturday while Cassandra waited for me on the porch with a pitcher of ice-cold lemonade.

Yeah, right. Cassandra wasn't exactly the waiting-on-the-porch-with-a-pitcher-of-lemonade type. And where was Melody in this fantasy? Nowhere. That said a lot. I guess she was back at the club, still trying to sell her dad's stolen coke.

Shit. Just like that, the bubble burst.

I stood up. I had work to do.

Walter sat in the gloom of his house. A life-size silver statue of a bald eagle descending on its prey sat on a side table beneath a mirror. Walter was collapsed on a black leather sofa. He looked like a pile of rumpled laundry. "Melody's not here."

I stared past him. His house was trashed. The sofa was all ripped up. Big heaps of stuffing puffed up from the cushions like smoke from a volcano. The coffee table was overturned, the glass broken, one leg missing. I reached down and plucked a photo from the rubble. Jagged shards of glass still clung to the frame. Walter and little Melody, seven or eight years old, her giant grown-up teeth all snaggly; a photo snapped in simpler times. The two of them hugging, laughing, wearing pastel sweatshirts and sunglasses with white frames. Behind them, a rainbow arched above Niagara Falls.

"What happened?"

Walter nudged a broken stool with the steel toe of his boot and then bent over and picked it up. "They fuckin' tossed the place, Jack. Melody was right upstairs." He shook his head. "They didn't know she was here. They came around the corner and she squeezed off four shots. Didn't hit anyone, but they cleared out quick."

"She's lucky she's alive. You're both lucky."

Walter glowered. "I don't feel so lucky. This is my home, Jack. I feel fucking violated."

I nodded. "I get that."

"First he shoots me in the stomach, and then he trashes my house."

"So you think this was Fisher?"

"Melody saw him, man. Said he was here looking for the coke." Walter stared off into space. "It used to be fun, you know? It used to be about riding and partying with your brothers. Then everybody became a fucking drug dealer." Fisher shook his head. "I bet Fisher doesn't even remember how to change a fucking tire."

I mimicked holding up a phone. "Hello, CAA?"

Walter blinked. Then he laughed. "You're a fucking trip, Jack. You know that?"

I walked across the ruined living room. At the front door, I paused. "This might not have been Fisher."

Walter squinted. "What do you mean? Melody saw him herself."

"Yeah, well, she might've been confused, adrenalin running high, shooting at figures in the dark. Hell, you're lucky she didn't shoot you."

Walter grunted. "That's me. Mr. Lucky."

"I'm going to talk to Melody. Do me a favour, Walter. Don't do anything drastic."

I drove to Melody's place. She knew I was coming, but she still wasn't ready. She rummaged through her little house, peeling clothes off the backs of dining room chairs. "How was it up north?"

"It was good." I paused. "I met someone."

"Oh yeah?" Melody grinned. "A love connection?"

"We spent the night together."

"Were you safe?"

"Always."

"C'mon," Melody said, taking my hand, "let's go for a drive."

———

I drove. Melody sat in the passenger seat holding her white leather purse in her lap.

"I went to see your dad tonight. His place was trashed."

"Fisher, man. He's looking for the coke."

"Don't lie to me, Mel."

"He wants his stuff, Jack — the stuff or the money."

"But you're not going to give it to him."

"Hell, no. Fuck him. He came up the stairs. I was scared shitless. I grabbed my dad's gun and rattled off four shots."

"You could've killed him."

"Shit, I wish I had."

"No, you don't." I took a sideways glance at Melody.

She frowned. "What? You think I could make something like that up?"

I didn't say anything. The car slid through the night.

Melody pointed. "Turn here."

I stopped the car in front of Riverdale Park East. We were on the top of a massive hill. Below us was the city skyline, lit up against the night. I glanced over at Melody. "We need to talk about the coke."

Melody hopped out of the car. "You'll have to catch me first." And then she was off, running through the grass, her blond ponytail flicking from side to side.

I jumped out and ran. I caught her, wrapping my arms around her waist. She squealed and pretended to struggle. Then she raised her left hand and pressed her palm against the side of my face. She raised her ruby-red lips to mine. I leaned in for the kiss and she broke away laughing.

"Seriously, Mel. The coke …"

She put her finger to her lips. "Shh."

She danced in front of me, flowing like quicksilver in the dark. "Can your Sauble Beach girl dance like this?" She tugged down her grey sweatpants and her hot-pink thong and waggled her ass at me. I reached out with both hands, grabbed her butt cheeks and squeezed. She moaned and bent over, pushing against my hands. I pushed back with one hand and unzipped my zipper. My penis jutted out into the cool night air. "Yes," she whispered. "Yes." She went down on her hands and knees on the damp grass. I slid two fingers into her warm, wet slit. She jolted as if hit by a bolt of electricity and then settled back against my hand. My body throbbed toward hers. I grabbed her hips, pulled her closer and thrust inside.

"Slow … slow …"

I pushed into her again, slower this time, in and out, slick against her skin. She groaned. I kept grasping her hip with my right hand. I reached under her shirt with my left hand and found the warm soft curve of her breast. I pinched her nipple, hard, as I pushed all the way inside. She gasped. I closed my eyes and rocked, slow at first but then faster, the smell of the damp grass, the coconut smell of her skin, the warm wet tightness of her pussy grasping me, the tingling feeling building up in my core, faster and faster and faster, both my hands clamping against her hips, and then I shoved all the way inside, trying to get every last bit of me inside of her. Her whole body shuddered. I shook like an earthquake as I came.

We lay gasping in the wet grass. The clouds twisted by, revealing the moon. She sat up and lit a cigarette. She exhaled and looked over at me and smiled. "Goddamn, Jack."

I sat up, too. "Give me one of those."

She leaned her head against my shoulder and we smoked, watching the full moon shine down over the heart of the city.

CHAPTER 41

I dropped Melody off at the club and then stopped by the liquor store on my way back home. Bottle after bottle, row after row. I bought a bottle of Jim Beam and six tallboys of Steam Whistle. Over by the door, a tired-looking man was being handcuffed by the cops. The man's hair, clothes, and skin were all the colour of dust. Busted for trying to boost some booze. The cops were wearing rubber gloves to protect themselves against bad blood. I watched as they led the dusty man out.

That wouldn't be me. My rock bottom would look different, I was sure of it. The Chief went out in a blaze of glory — sex and booze and drugs — one final hurrah before a hit man cut him down. That's the kind of rock bottom that was waiting for me. Or maybe I'd get hit by a bus tomorrow. Who the fuck knows?

Back in my office, I soaked my grass-stained pants in some hot water and dish soap in my bathroom sink, but the green didn't wash out. When I was a kid, Mom and I washed all our clothes in dish soap, making that long trek to the laundromat with all our clothes bundled up in black garbage bags. Dish soap is about five times cheaper than laundry soap, but it doesn't get clothes as clean; no matter how many times we washed them, the clothes still smelled slightly funky. The only reason I was soaking my pants in dish soap now was because I was out of laundry soap. That's right, these days I used actual laundry soap because I was a real high roller.

There was a knock on the door. I spotted Eddie through the peephole and slid the bolts and popped the locks.

Eddie glanced down at the beer can in my hand and then up at me. "Can I come in?"

I nodded and stepped out of the way. The big man inched past me into the stale air of the office. "Cassandra's down in the casino. She's grinding it out, Jack. She's playing poker like someone's got a gun to her head."

"Is she winning?"

"Up and down, Jack. Up and down." Eddie shuffled over to the sofa and plopped himself down. Something inside the sofa creaked. He ran his hand along the blue velour. "Do you remember the night you burned your old couch?"

I finished off the beer and nodded.

"Do you remember what happened after you burned it?"

I squinted, trying to cast my mind back. What had happened? I stood swaying in the alley and I watched the couch burn. And then what? In my mind I did a victory lap complete with streamers, confetti, and a roaring crowd. I remembered waking up the next morning on the floor, staring over at the dirty rectangle where the couch had sat. Dust bunnies, spare change, bottle caps, and smudges of random grime.

Eddie shifted his bulk. "I was in my office. I glanced up at my security feed and I saw your drunk ass dragging that old couch into the alley. *Good*, I thought. *He's finally throwing that ratty old thing out.* But then you started flicking that Zippo. I thought, *What the fuck?*" Eddie shook his head and chuckled. "You got that thing going pretty good. Those old couches burn, man. I came running out with Josh and Vin. They doused that shit with fire extinguishers while I held you back. Your face was all twisted up like a Halloween mask. 'Let it burn!' you kept shouting. 'Let that shit burn!'"

I nodded. "That couch had to go."

Eddie leaned forward, the couch creaking. "Can you see any problem with burning a couch directly outside an illegal motherfucking casino?"

I opened my mouth and shut it.

Eddie kept staring at me. "I didn't say anything at the time because I could see you were hurting. And we got that fire out quick. The next day I got some guys to haul that shit to the dump. No harm, no foul. But goddamn, Jack. If the cops had come …"

"You pay the cops."

"Some of them, sure. But I don't have a magic money tree. I can't pay *all* the cops." Eddie sighed. He ran his hand through his hair. "I'm just saying. I like to have a drink every now and then. But I know my limits. Even better, I respect them. You and I have had a lot of good fun drinking. Don't get me started. But at some point maybe the drinking starts to do more harm than good." Eddie creaked to his feet. "Do me a favour, will you? Think about it."

CHAPTER 42

The next morning I cracked my eyes open and wondered if maybe Eddie had a point. I splashed cold water on my face, and then I slumped on the couch until my brain came back online. This hangover routine was getting old.

I drove out to see Fisher. Maybe the old biker really had trashed Walter's place. It was hard to picture Melody smashing up her own dad's house. Then again, I wouldn't put it past her.

Fisher was in his cracked driveway, standing next to his old brown station wagon. His old German shepherd, Brutus, was sitting on the passenger seat. Fisher frowned as I pulled up to the curb. "Mornin', Jack. You're up bright and early."

"Heard you paid a visit to Walter the other night."

"I don't know who told you that, but the other night I was right here taking care of my sick ol' dog." Fisher reached in through the window and gave Brutus a pat. "Isn't that right, boy?"

"Your dog is your alibi."

"I don't need a motherfucking alibi. I didn't do shit."

I waited but Fisher didn't say anything else. Finally, the biker sighed. "Car won't start. Drive us to the vet, will you, Jack?"

Fisher sat in the passenger seat with his arm around the dog. Brutus was panting, looking through the windshield with his one good eye. The other eye was cloudy and white. The dog smelled terrible.

"Cassie's got to come back to Anton, Jack."

"It's not going to happen."

"He wants his money." Fisher stared through the windshield. "I can't stall him forever." Fisher pointed. "Turn here," he said.

The vet's office was a little ivy-covered brick building on King Street just north of the Distillery District. I pulled in behind the building and then turned into a parking lot. I cut the engine and the three of us just sat there staring through the windshield like we were casing the joint.

I got out and breathed deep. All that big dog funk in one little car.

Fisher climbed out, too, stumbling and almost falling down onto the asphalt. "Brutus, come!"

The big dog bounded out of the car and went sprawling on the pavement. Fisher caught his collar and pulled him back to his feet. "Arthritis. He don't move so good anymore." He reached into his pocket and pulled out a fistful of doggie treats. Brutus lapped them up gratefully, eating right out of Fisher's hand.

Fisher looked up. "Even on death row, you get a last meal."

"Shit, I'm sorry."

"We had a good run, didn't we, boy?"

Brutus thumped his tail.

Fisher turned and headed for the veterinarian, and the old dog followed.

At the front door, Brutus whined and stopped. Fisher bent down and ruffled the dog's fur while he whispered in his ear. I glanced up and down the street.

"So, uh, I'll wait for you in the car."

I left Fisher on the vet's stoop, hugging his dog.

I didn't get back in the car. I leaned against it instead, breathing the air and feeling the sun against my face. The sunlight filtering through the trees was making shadows dance across the pavement. I wondered what my last meal would be, when my time came.

After about half an hour, I had to pee. I could piss behind the building, but it was broad daylight and cars and people were going by. I'd peed in plenty of alleyways in my time, but only when I was drunk. Right now I was sober and I didn't want to get busted for something as stupid as urinating in public.

I walked back into the vet's and smiled at the receptionist. "Is there a bathroom?"

"Down the hall. Third door on the right."

"Thanks."

"Wait! You'll need the key."

How do you spell relief? I zipped up, washed my hands, and headed back into the hallway. Fisher was down the hall, head down, leaning against a wall.

He saw me coming and straightened up, brushing away a tear. "That's that. He was a damn good dog."

"I'm sorry, Fisher."

"Yeah, well …" Fisher shrugged. "Circle of life and all that, right?" He pulled a red bandana out of his back pocket and blew his nose. He tucked the bandana back into his pocket and without looking at me, turned and headed for the exit.

CHAPTER 43

"He's having a what?"

"A wake. A funeral for his dog."

Cassandra frowned. "Did he kill his dog?"

"No. Well, sort of. He had him put down."

Eddie's casino buzzed around us. "I always figured Fisher would be the type of guy to put down his own dog. Take it for one last romp in the woods and then pull the trigger."

"Yeah, well … it's not that easy."

Cassandra sipped her gin and tonic and then set the glass down on the bar. "I've got to get back to work."

"You're grinding."

"Hell yeah, I'm grinding. I owe Anton six hundred grand and now I owe Freddy a hundred grand, too." Cassandra tugged at her sleeve, subconsciously trying to pull it over her hand. "I can't sleep. I can barely eat. I might as well play. Try to build up my chip stack."

"How's that going?"

"You should've seen the hand I had yesterday, Jack. Beautiful flush, all diamonds."

"And today?"

Cassandra stood up. "Today's not over."

I watched her head over to the tables. I turned and signalled for one more drink.

The back door of the casino burst open. Two skinny guys in black hoodies and BMX masks ran into the room with pistols in their hands. "Get your hands up. GET 'EM UP!" The men in masks were so nervous they were shaking. "The money. COME ON, MOTHERFUCKERS! THE MONEY!"

Eddie kicked open the door of his office and came out shooting. One of the robbers jerked and twitched. A red bloom was spreading on his hoodie. The other robber screamed, dropped his gun, and ran for the back door.

Eddie cracked off another shot. The second robber stiffened and fell. The sound of the gunshots was deafening inside the close confines of the basement. Everyone in the casino ducked for cover. Someone was screaming.

Holding his gun with both hands, Eddie cautiously approached the bodies sprawled out on the floor. Blood pooled on the casino carpet. Eddie knelt down, pulled back the robber's hoodie and peeled back the mask. A young teenager, fifteen, maybe sixteen, stared up at him. "Fuck."

Eddie stood up and handed his pistol to Vin. Vin turned and headed out the door. The guns would be wiped and dumped in a storm sewer.

Eddie lashed out and kicked over a chair. "FUCK!"

I tried to put my arm around Eddie, but he raised his shoulder and butted my arm away.

Four of Eddie's guys stepped forward and picked up the bodies and dragged them from the room.

Eddie stumped over and plopped himself down at the bar. Vivian put a full glass of Scotch in front of him and gave his arm a pat. He drank deep and then looked up at me. "Just kids, Jack. Just a couple of goddamn kids."

The casino had cleared out pretty fast. No one wanted to stick around after the shooting. Cassandra still sat by herself at one of the poker tables, flipping her chips from one hand to the other. Vin worked a carpet cleaner. I walked over to Eddie's office and knocked on the door.

The only light on in Eddie's office was the pale-orange glow of his desk lamp. A haze of smoke hung in the air. Eddie inhaled half a cigarette in one pull. He exhaled and the haze shifted and twisted, smoke merging and breaking apart. "You okay?"

Eddie didn't say anything. He puffed and exhaled. "I was robbed before, back when I was just starting out. Two guys, not kids, old-time stick-up men. Someone had tipped them off that there was a new kid in town. Back then we didn't even have the roulette wheel yet. It was all poker. We had five rickety card tables plus the bar. I built that bar myself." Eddie flashed me a crooked grin. "No one plays roulette in an underground basement casino. But I wanted the place to look, you know, classy. I wanted it to look real. Someone comes in, I want them to be transported. I want them to feel special.

I want them to feel like James fucking Bond standing in a casino in Monte Carlo. So I added the wheel. But the first time I was robbed, it didn't look like Monte Carlo. The bar itself, that was beautiful. Solid oak, sanded and stained — five coats of stain on that sucker. Sand, stain, sand, stain, and so on and so forth. I mean, that sucker practically glowed. But other than the bar, the place looked like shit. It looked like a bunch of gangsters hunched over rickety-ass card tables playing poker in the basement."

Eddie lit another cigarette off the first one's last dying embers. "So these guys come in. I had a young kid, Slim, watching the door. The gunmen marched him in with his hands by his sides. Vin was over by the bar. He started to go for his gun but I waved him off. I didn't want anyone getting hurt." Eddie shook his head slowly. "Those two punks stripped us bare. They even took my fucking Rolex. But money, watches ... stuff can be replaced. Life, though ... once it's gone, it's gone for good."

Eddie shifted in his office chair. The cigarette smouldered between his fingers. "Aunt Cecilia had fronted me some start-up cash and she was a silent partner in my whole thing. The punks who robbed us didn't know that, but they found out. David — you know him, Aunt Cecilia's oldest, David the Dragon — found those guys. We got our money back, but at that point it wasn't even about the money."

Eddie exhaled in a slow, steady stream, blowing smoke toward the ceiling. "Aunt Cecilia said we had to send a message." Eddie took another drag. "One of those punks just disappeared. They didn't find his body then and they're not going to find it now. The other guy, they found him in his boarding house. His landlady found him, or at least most of him. His head and hands were left on the floor of his bedroom. One hand, palm down, on either side of his severed head. Just sitting on those dusty boarding-house floorboards." Eddie shook his head. "That was some gruesome shit. But Aunt Cecilia got her point across. Word spread and no one fucked with us again. Now and then some asshole tries to palm some chips, but a smack across the knuckles with a hammer usually puts a stop to that. And when King Diamond tried to muscle his way in …" Eddie stubbed out his cigarette. "But we took care of that, didn't we? And now this." Eddie took a big swig of Scotch. "This was a test run, Jack. There's folks who have been waiting in the wings for Cecilia to drop dead. Now that she's gone, they're going to come out of the woodwork, trying to stake their claim."

CHAPTER 44

Cassandra and I sat side by side on my new couch. She was drinking a beer and I was holding a club soda. I wanted to kiss her. I wanted to do more than that. I looked her in the eye and then I leaned in. She leaned away. I got the message.

I straightened up and drank the club soda. The bubbles burned my nose.

"You know the real reason I left, Jack?"

I waited.

Cassandra sighed. "You were violent, sure, but never toward me. You were distant — emotionally distant. But that's not why I left, either."

"So what, then?"

"I had to figure some stuff out." Cassie looked up. "I like women, Jack."

I blinked.

"I always have." Cassandra looked away. "In high school, I tried to pretend I didn't. I dated guys. Some of them I even liked. I liked you, Jack. But you were hardly ever around." She smiled. "I think that was part of the appeal."

I nodded. "Thanks for telling me. I'm glad you trust me." I raised my glass. "Mazel tov."

Cassandra looked at me from the corner of her eyes. "There's something else."

"Oh yeah?"

"Is Melody bisexual?"

I sat there without moving.

"You said you're not exclusive. She's bi, right?"

I nodded.

"Maybe I'll ask her out. After all this shit with Anton is over." Cassandra bit her nails and stared at me. "What do you think about that?"

I stood up. "I think Melody is like that person at the circus with all the spinning plates. Sooner or later, one of those plates is going to break."

I kept it civil. If there's one thing I've learned over the years, it's this: leave things civil with the folks you care about. You never know what's waiting around the corner. The last thing The Chief ever said to me was "Fuck you." It shouldn't still sting, but it did. It stung when I pictured him there scowling in that motel room surrounded by empty bottles. He didn't know it then, but he was at the end of his string. Or maybe he did know and that's why he was trying to soak up all the booze in the goddamn world. Shit, I'm one to talk.

I headed out into the cool night air and the sound of sirens. City sounds. After a while, you don't even notice the sirens anymore.

CHAPTER 45

Moonlight sparkled on Ashbridges Bay. The ember of Freddy Johns's cigar glowed orange in the darkness. "Here's how I see it, Jack. It's almost over." We strolled through the trees. To our right, across the bike path, was a park. Past the park was sand, and in the distance was the blackness of the lake.

"I appreciate all your efforts, Freddy."

"It's time to put this Tommy shit to bed." Freddy puffed his cigar. "Then there's that other thing."

"Cassandra."

"Yeah." The big man squinted. The moonlight shone down through the trees. "You know me, Jack. I'm a reasonable man. Let her know I'll give her a payment plan that makes sense. For her, I'll lower my usual rates."

The interest on the hundred grand Cassie owed Freddy would still be punishing. He'd lower his rates from highway robbery down to regular old robbery.

We shook hands. "I appreciate it, Freddy."

"Hey," Freddy said, grinning, "what are friends for?" He turned back to look at the lake. That's when Grover stepped out of the trees and slit the big man's throat.

The next day I headed back to the lake. Freddy's body had been carted off sometime last night. Four little kids were playing with the police caution tape. They'd torn it down and were laughing as they wound themselves all up in it. I looked around but their parents were elsewhere, grilling meat, drinking beer. It was a beautiful day.

The crime tech guys had taken their photos. The homicide guys had made notes in their little notebooks. I didn't see any of that, but I knew that's how it worked. They would be interviewing witnesses, too. Anyone see the fat man strolling through the trees puffing on a cigar while he chatted with a friend? I turned and headed toward the parking lot. A sparrow lifted off from a nearby tree. The children shouted and danced, yellow caution tape dangling from their arms like ribbons.

CHAPTER 46

Without Freddy going to bat for me with the council, Sammy DiAngelo would push them the other way. The shot would be called and another hit man would be on his way. Grover thought he was helping, but he had fucked me good. Cassie getting off the hook for a hundred grand was the silver lining, but Sammy and his friends were still after me. Plus she still owed Anton six hundred large. He wouldn't be patient forever.

I stood in Eddie's casino and I watched Cassandra play a few hands. Her chip stack grew. I headed up the stairs. If I timed it right, I could get to Melody's house soon after her shift ended.

I timed it wrong. I went around the corner to a little place on Queen and had a coffee. I tried to read a magazine, but my eyes kept skimming off the page. I stared out the window. It was a rare treat just to sit and do nothing. Then I stood up and went back to Melody's.

When she threw open the door, she was wearing a robe and had a beer in her hand. "How's it going, Jack?"

I followed her inside. "Cassandra told me she was thinking of asking you out."

"Really?" Melody smiled. "Well, isn't that something?"

"I don't know about this, Mel."

She put her hand on her hip. "Why not? You had your Sauble Beach girl, right? If it's safe and consensual, then I'm all for it. I like sex, Jack. I'm going to hop in the shower. Stick around, will you? You can give me a ride to my dad's house."

"You gonna tell him about the coke?"

Melody laughed. "What coke?"

She sauntered into the bathroom and closed the door. I heard the water running. I walked over to the living room window and peered out into the street. No motorcycles. I looked over at the front door. Then I sat down and closed my eyes.

"Hey, Jack! You still here?"

I stood up and walked into the hall. Melody stepped out of the bathroom. She was wearing white cotton panties and nothing else. Her blond hair was still damp from the shower. She pointed to a white laundry basket on the floor. "Hand me that towel, will you?"

I did. The polite thing to do would be to stop staring at her breasts. I didn't. Her nipples looked like raspberries. I wanted to bite them.

She's bad news, Jack.

Yeah, but, you know, on the other hand …

Melody wrapped the white towel around her head like a turban. She smiled at me and then headed toward the bedroom. I watched her go. Beneath her thin cotton panties, her buttocks swayed from side to side as she sauntered down the hall.

Come on, Jack. Stay away.

Yeah, but —

"There's Scotch in the kitchen," Melody called over her shoulder. "Help yourself."

"I've got to go."

She stopped and smiled. "You say that, but you're still here." Her breasts jiggled as she put her hands on her hips. "Come on, Jack. Have a drink with me."

I glanced into the kitchen. The bottle was right there, glowing amber beneath the kitchen lights. Melody was walking toward me, half naked. I turned away from the bottle and stared into Melody's eyes. "Goodbye, Mel."

CHAPTER 47

Melody wasn't going to come clean. She was going to cling stubbornly to her delusion of a Cocaine Empire, even if it meant driving her dad straight into an open grave. Fisher wasn't going to quit until either he or Walter was dead in the ground.

I waited in Melody's living room until she took a cab to her dad's house and then I called Marcus. He told me where to look. In Melody's basement was a storage room full of clothes, and in the corner of the storage room was a big cardboard box. I reached out with my huge hands and I pushed her clothes aside. Then I moved the box. On the floor of the basement where the box had been was a small metal hatch. The feathers from her angel costume tickled my nose as I knelt down and lifted the covering off the hatch. Underneath was a small dark hole that might've held a sump pump at one point. The sump pump was gone, and instead, a dark green duffle bag sat in the darkness. I reached in and fished it out.

When I unzipped the bag, there it was — four kilos of uncut cocaine, wrapped in plastic. One of the bags had been cut open. Either Melody or Marcus had dipped into it. Maybe Melody had scooped up some to sell at the club or maybe the powder had gone right up her nose. Frankly, I didn't care one way or another. She'd had plenty of chances to come clean and she blew each one.

I zipped the duffle bag shut and carried it out of the storage room.

I took the coke and drove to Walter's. Fisher was standing in the living room and Melody was sitting on the couch. Walter stood reeling in the doorway, a gun dangling from his hand. The big biker was fucked right up. Pills? Booze? Leapers? Screamers? Reefer? All of the above? He stumbled as he loaded his pistol.

I stepped into the house. "Give me the gun, Walter."

Walter turned toward me and squinted. "Fuck you. Fuck off. Go fuck yourself. This is my gun."

"Come on, Walter. Let's get a drink, you and me."

Walter slammed the last bullet into the pistol. He turned and looked at me, closing one eye to bring me into focus. "Who the fuck are you? Fuck off. I got shit to do."

Fisher spread his arms. "You gonna shoot us all, Walter? Plug me right in the belly? Go right ahead."

Walter waved the gun around. "I should. I should fucking shoot you like you shot me. I told you, I don't have the fucking coke. Now get the fuck out of my house."

"Dad —"

"Go home, Melody."

I glanced over at Melody. *Last chance to come clean*, I thought. She caught my eye and then looked away.

Walter scowled at Fisher. The pistol swayed in his hand. "I said get out!"

Fisher nodded. "All right. But this isn't over." Fisher turned and stomped out the door.

I watched him go and then stepped forward and dropped the duffle bag onto the coffee table with a satisfying thud. "There's the coke. Four kilos, more or less."

Walter cocked his head, puzzled. Gears were turning inside his brain. "You took my shit?"

I kept my eye on the gun in his hand. "Nope. I found it in Melody's house."

Walter blinked. "It was you?"

"Dad …"

"It was you." Walter's shoulders sagged. "This whole time. This whole time, it was you."

I stepped forward and closed my hand around Walter's gun. He gave it up without a fight. I walked over and put the pistol on the dining room table.

"Dad, wait. It's not like that."

"No? What the fuck is it like?"

Melody plastered a huge smile across her face. "I was going to split the money. You would've gotten your cut. I just didn't want to see you get hurt."

Walter didn't say anything. Then he looked at Melody. The big biker looked weary, as if he had been riding for a thousand miles. "Get out."

"Dad, wait."

Walter looked over at me. "I keep throwing people out of my house, but nobody's listening."

"Knock, knock." Fisher stood in the doorway with a shotgun. He grinned. "I'll take the coke." He levelled the shotgun at Walter.

Walter's fist closed around the straps of the duffle bag. "Are you kidding me? Fuck that."

Melody clutched her father's arm. "Dad, just give him the shit."

Walter shook her off. "Fuck that and fuck you. Did you trash my house, too?" He looked up at Fisher. "She blamed you, you know. Can you believe that shit?"

"Yeah," Fisher said. "I can." He jabbed out with the shotgun. "Slide the bag over, Walter."

"Dad, just do it."

"Give it to him, Walter."

Fisher kept grinning. "Listen to them, Walter. Don't make me shoot you again."

Eyes full of hate, Walter shoved the duffle bag across the coffee table. He turned his head and spit on his own floor. "We had a dream, you and me. What the fuck went wrong?"

CHAPTER 48

"Fisher."

"Shut up."

"Look, man —"

Fisher reached out and smashed me in the nose with the butt of his pistol. I saw white and then I saw red. It hurt like hell. He kept his left hand on the wheel and grimaced. "Goddamn it, Jack, I thought we were friends. You're gonna turn around and give Walter my shit?"

I held my hand to my nose. I was pretty sure it was broken. Blood gushed through my fingers. Fisher kept talking. "And you didn't even come to my dog's funeral. You know Brutus would've wanted you there. That shit stung, Jack."

Fisher had held me at gunpoint back at Walter's house while I removed my knives. I left them all on the big biker's coffee table. Hopefully they would still be there when I got back. If I got back. "Where are we going?" My voice was muffled by my hand full of blood.

"Time's up, Jack. We're going to get Cassandra."

"Leave her out of this."

"Oh, she's in it. She's fucking all the way in this shit right here."

The old biker had gotten his station wagon up and running again. The shotgun was on the back seat, right next to the duffle bag full of cocaine. I could see the gun resting on the seat in the rear-view. Fisher followed my eyes and chuckled. "Thought you didn't like guns. You just be cool, Jack. This is almost over. You help me load up Cassie and then we'll all pay Anton a friendly visit."

"I told you, Anton will get his money."

"Yeah, you told me. And I told Anton. But guess what? He's still sitting on a big pile of nothing."

"How can you work for that man?"

Fisher was quiet for a minute. He turned the wheel and the station wagon cut left. "There's lots of bad bosses out there, Jack. I bet you've worked for a few."

I thought about Tommy and I kept my mouth shut.

Fisher peered through the windshield. "Anton is a means to an end. I wasn't gonna involve him in this coke business. I figured I could make more if Walter sold the shit instead of Anton." He shook his head. "That was a fucking mistake. I should've known Walter would fuck it up six ways till Sunday. So, I'll take what I can get from Anton. Wholesale, yeah, but every bit counts."

"You really think you're going to bring back Satan's Blood?"

Fisher laughed. "You gotta have a dream, Jack. If you don't have a dream, you're already dead."

At a red light, Fisher kept the pistol levelled on me while he pulled a cellphone out of his pocket. He tossed the phone onto my lap. "Call Cassie. Tell her to meet us at the southeast corner of Queen and Spadina."

"No."

"What?" There was a menacing growl in Fisher's voice.

"She doesn't want anything to do with Anton. Not anymore."

Fisher frowned. "You gotta understand my position here, Jack. Anton might have his faults, sure, but he's my boss. He says go get Cassie, well then, I go get Cassie."

"That simple, huh?"

"That's right. Just that fucking simple."

"You're a good soldier."

"Damn right."

"You're just following orders."

Fisher scowled. "Watch it." Fisher gestured with his gun. "Call her. No funny business or I'll shoot you right in your motherfucking head."

I could see Fisher was right on the edge. I punched in Cassandra's number. She answered. "Hello?"

"Meet me at the southeast corner of Queen and Spadina in five minutes. We're on our way."

"Jack? Is everything all right?"

I didn't say anything.

"Who's 'we'? Who's with you?"

I still didn't say anything. On the other end of the phone, Cassie exhaled. "It's him, isn't it? Fisher."

"Yes. We'll be there in five minutes."

"I'll be there."

"No."

There was silence on the other end of the line. Then Cassandra said, "I'm tired, Jack. Let's just get this done."

I glanced over at Fisher. The old biker was distracted by traffic. With one hand I grabbed the barrel of his gun and twisted. With the other hand I smashed him in the face with his phone. Fisher cursed and slammed on the brakes. The station wagon tires screeched against the street. Another light turned red. Blood was gushing down his face. I pointed the gun right at him, holding it low so the drivers behind us couldn't see it. A nose for a nose. The pain in my nose had died down to a dull throb.

Fisher glared at me. "You're making a mistake."

"Wouldn't be the first time." The light turned green. I gestured with the gun. "Keep driving."

I kept the gun fixed on Fisher as we drove. "Cassandra is sick of running from Anton. She wants to put this all behind her. But we're going to do this my way."

Fisher glanced over at the gun in my fist. "Just be careful, man. That trigger is real sensitive."

I wanted to roll down the window and chuck the gun out onto the street. But then the gun might go off and an innocent person might get shot. I wasn't about to let that happen.

Fisher glanced over at me again. "So what's the plan here, Jack? You gonna march me up to Anton at gunpoint? He's going to see that shit on his security cameras and you won't even get past the front door."

I saw Cassandra up ahead standing on the corner of the busy intersection. "Pull over."

"I'm just saying, let's talk about this."

Cassandra climbed into the back. She blinked when she saw me holding the gun. "Jack?"

I kept my eyes fixed on Fisher. "You know me, Cassie. I get a little itchy when someone tries to hold me at gunpoint."

Cassie stared at me and then stared at Fisher. "It smells like blood in here."

I nodded. "Yeah. Do me a favour, will you? Put the shotgun in the duffle bag with the coke."

"Easy, though," Fisher said. "That gun's a collector's item. It was machined from a single solid block of American steel."

"Shut up, Fisher," I said. "Nobody cares."

CHAPTER 49

We headed south on Spadina toward Anton's penthouse at Queen's Quay. Fisher punched in a code and the parking garage doors rumbled up. The car slid down the ramp like a minnow disappearing into the mouth of a great white shark.

Fisher pulled into a parking spot and we all piled out. The gun was in my hand and my hand was in my jacket pocket. Cassie carried the bag.

We took the elevator up to the penthouse. Fisher knocked once and opened the door. We all filed in. Beside me I could feel Cassandra shivering.

Inside, the penthouse was opulent. The carpet was lush white shag. Anton's furniture was black leather and chrome. The man himself sat behind a massive mahogany desk in front of a giant wall of glass. Beyond the glass was the lake. He smiled when he saw us walk in.

"Welcome back, Cassie."

Cassandra looked away. Her face was red.

Fisher frowned. "He's got a gun, Boss."

Anton stood up from behind his massive desk. There was a sleek black .45 in his fist. "I figured. Get that gun out of your pocket, Mr. Palace."

I didn't move. Anton kept smiling. "Are you a good shot? Maybe you can shoot me before I shoot you, maybe not. Can you shoot both me and Fisher before one of us kills Cassie? Is that a gamble you're willing to take?" Anton dropped his smile. His eyes were cold and grey like slate. "Drop the fucking gun."

I did. It thudded into the white shag. I was hoping maybe it would go off and shoot Anton in the head but it didn't.

Fisher stepped toward me, his hands curled into fists. I braced myself.

"No!" Anton barked. Fisher froze. Anton shook his head. "You come in close, he's going to break your arm. Aren't you, Jack?"

I didn't say anything. Fisher glared at me then turned and walked across the carpet toward Cassie. He took the bag from her, opened it up and pulled out the shotgun. Fisher grinned at me. "Don't need to get close now."

Fisher tossed the bag onto Anton's massive mahogany desk. Still keeping the gun on me, Anton gave the bag a pat. "Is this what I think it is?"

Fisher nodded. "Four keys of uncut, more or less. We can sell this shit ourselves. Take a bit of profit, then channel the rest into bringing back the Blood."

Anton stared at Fisher. "I'm keeping the coke." He smiled as he wrapped his hand around the duffle bag straps. His teeth were perfect. "Call it a finder's fee."

Fisher blinked. I could see his knuckles turn white around the shotgun. "Finder's fee? I brought you that shit."

"And I thank you." Still keeping his left hand on the straps, Anton levelled the .45 at me and Cassandra. "Cassie, take a seat. You're going to be here a while."

She stood still like a statue. Then she shook her head. "No." Her voice was quiet, disbelieving.

Fisher stepped forward. His hands were still white-knuckled around the shotgun. "We were going to bring back the Blood. We had a deal. You promised me, Boss."

"I had a talk with my friends in the Angels. They agreed that bringing back Satan's Blood wasn't the best idea after all."

"But…" Fisher spluttered. The shotgun trembled in his grasp.

Anton's left eyebrow shot up. His gun was still levelled at Cassie and me. "Fisher, stay cool, now."

"You fucking promised!" Fisher whipped up the shotgun. Anton swept the .45 toward Fisher and fired.

The old biker staggered and plopped down on the white shag with his back propped against the wall. The shotgun slipped from Fisher's hands. Blood began to pool beneath him.

That's going to leave a stain, I thought stupidly.

Keeping an eye on Anton, I took a step toward the shotgun. Anton was looking at Fisher with an almost idle curiosity, as if Fisher were a fly and Anton had just pulled off his wings. I reached for the shotgun, but Cassandra got there first. In one fluid motion she scooped it up and fired. She screamed as she pulled the trigger. Anton's chest exploded. He looked surprised. The floor to ceiling window behind him shattered. Cassandra fired the other barrel. This time her aim was a little off and the duffle bag exploded. White powder went everywhere. Anton reeled, hand still clutching the bag. Eyes wide with surprise, he tumbled back through the window, falling through a cloud of cocaine and broken glass.

The wind rushed in. Cassandra stared, unblinking, at the broken window and the spot where Anton had been just seconds ago.

"Give me the gun, Cassie."

Behind us, Fisher gurgled. I knew at a glance it was all over for the old biker. His arms and legs twitched as he died.

"Cassie! The gun!"

Cassie blinked and handed me the gun. The barrels were hot to the touch. I threw the gun across Anton's office and then I swept her up in my arms.

CHAPTER 50

We sat in my office with all the shades drawn. The light from my desk lamp cast a murky orange glow. Cassandra sat on the couch, a glass of Scotch in her hand. She stared straight ahead at nothing. I was sitting next to her, but at a respectful distance.

Finally, she said, "I thought I would feel better." She glanced over at me and smiled her crooked half smile. "I thought about this day for a long, long time. I used to lie awake at night and think of all the ways I could kill Anton. It was almost like counting sheep. Poison … shooting … stabbing …" She closed her eyes and a single tear rolled down her cheek. "Now I close my eyes and I can still see him falling. Right out that window, Jack. Just like my mom."

"Don't even think it."

"What's the difference, Jack?" Cassie hung her head. "I'm just like him. Just like my fucking dad."

"No." I reached out and put my hand on her arm. "Here's the difference. Anton was a monster. The world's better off without him."

"So why do I feel so bad?"

My phone buzzed. I glanced down at the text. "It's Melody. She wants to meet."

"She turned me down, you know."

"What?"

Cassandra turned away. "I asked her out. She said no."

"I'm sorry, Cassie."

She shrugged. "These things happen. Maybe I'm better off, right?"

The mist hung low over Withrow Park. My feet squelched through the wet grass as I walked toward the woman in the blue-and-white striped hoodie sitting hunched on top of a picnic table. She had her back to me but I knew it was her. "Melody?"

She didn't turn around. "Hi, Jack."

I walked over to the other side of the picnic table. I heard dogs barking in the dog park on the other side of the hill. A guy all done up like the Tour de France rolled by on his bike and then was swallowed by the fog.

Melody had been crying. Her tears had smudged her makeup, leaving black rings around her eyes. Her dyed blond bangs were wet from the mist. She stayed hunched over, hands shoved in her pockets, hood up. "You want a cigarette?"

I shook my head. "No thanks."

She pulled out a pack of smokes and shook one out, then sat there with it dangling from her mouth. Was she waiting for me to light it? After about twenty seconds she sighed, pulled out a tiny pink plastic lighter, and sparked it up herself.

"You all right?"

"No." Melody rubbed her eyes. "Not really. My dad's not talking to me, Jack."

"Can you blame him?"

"He's all I've got, Jack." She exhaled smoke into the mist. "I thought I was helping."

"No, you didn't. You thought he was a mark. You think everyone is a mark. Like me."

She shook her head. "No." She took one more puff and then ground out the cigarette on the top of the table. "I'm getting out of here."

"Yeah?"

"Yeah. Fuck it, I'm out." Melody snuffled and wiped her nose with the back of her sleeve. "I'm just going to pack up my shit and go. Just head off into the sunset. Move to Vermont, open up a bed and breakfast."

"Vermont, huh?"

"Sure, why not? Put little doilies around. Get some brass pots and antique teakettles. Lay in a supply of quilts and syrup. You like pancakes, right?"

"Everybody likes pancakes."

"Well, there you go." Melody looked up at me. Her eyes were wet but she was smiling. "Will you come stay at my bed and breakfast?"

I sat down beside her but didn't say anything.

She wiped her eyes. "Pancakes, Jack. Sounds pretty nice, right?"

We were both quiet for a minute, together in the mist.

"It might take a little while to get that bed and breakfast up and running."

"Yeah, it might." Melody leaned against my arm. "I'm still getting out of here, though. My dad has a cabin. We used to go there when I was little. He taught me how to fish …" She broke down sobbing, great heaving, painful sobs.

I turned and reached out for her. She slumped sideways into my arms. "I'm tired, Jack." Her voice sounded like a shipwreck, distant and drowning.

I patted her back and then stood up.

"Goodbye, Melody."

CHAPTER 51

Eddie and I strolled along the boardwalk by the beach. A family of four zipped by on bicycles. A blue-and-yellow-striped kite fluttered in the sky.

"You heard from Cassandra?"

"Yeah. I'm thinking of giving her a job." Eddie rolled the toothpick around his mouth. Twenty-two days without cigarettes. Almost a full month. "You cool with that?"

I nodded. "Sure."

"She might stay in your old office." Eddie smiled. "Be nice to have someone in there who actually cleans the place every now and then."

"You think she's tidy?" I shook my head. "You've been misinformed, my friend. She's not tidy at all."

"Well, then I guess nothing changes." Eddie stopped talking and we stood there quietly. The sun was shining. From a nearby tree, a bird began to sing.

He clapped me on the shoulder. "So long, Jack. Don't be a stranger."

CHAPTER 52

Make a break. Change your life. More and more, I was beginning to think it was possible. I got out of my brand-new truck and looked out into the fields. A cool breeze ruffled my hair. Birds were singing in a nearby tree. I had no idea what kind they were. There were thousands of different birds and I had no idea what they were all about. I knew city birds — sparrows, robins, pigeons, gulls, now and then blue jays and cardinals. Once in Melody's backyard I even saw a woodpecker. I heard it before I saw it, the hollow rapid-fire rat-tat-tat that made me think of cartoon gangsters with Tommy guns. And all the psychotic cartoon birds of my youth: Woody, Daffy, Donald. Once my mom threw our TV out the window of our fourth-floor apartment. "You sit glued to that thing like a fucking idiot!" she'd yelled. I'd run and hidden in my closet, crouched in the darkness, shaking while she raged.

Birds, man. I could see it now, sitting out here every morning with a pair of binoculars, steam rising from my cup of coffee. I could get one of those illustrated books about birds and just sit out here and watch the little fuckers bounce around. You ever see a bird walk? They hop, man. They hop and they bounce and on occasion they even strut.

Out here were fields, rolling green, stretching out toward the woods on the horizon. Overhead, clouds twisted by, taking their time. Time was different out here in the country. Once when I was lying low in The Chief's trailer, I realized that Einstein was right: time is relative. It took me three days to come down from City Time and sink deep into Country Time like it was a nice warm bath. It was quiet, man. No sirens, no gunshots. No hobos fighting in the alley. Don't get me wrong, I knew all kinds of horrendous shit went on behind closed doors. People were still people, and some shit never changed. But out here, in the clean country air, change seemed possible. And at night, you could see the stars.

Marcus walked over, grinning. I shook his hand. "I got the wood."

We walked back to the truck together. On the side it said PALACE SECURITY. The truck bed was filled with new boards for the barn. We would need more, but this was a good start.

We unloaded the wood, and we started to build.

ACKNOWLEDGEMENTS

Big thanks to my agent, Kelvin Kong of K2 Literary. Thanks as well to Sam Hiyate at The Rights Factory.

Thanks to Scott Fraser, Allison Hirst, Laura Boyle, Jenny McWha, and everyone else at Dundurn, as well as Catharine Chen, for helping turn my manuscript into a full-fledged book.

Thanks to the crew from The Old Neighbourhood: Iain Deans, Chris Turner, Beau Levitt, Julia Chan, Jason Lapeyre, Saira Hassan, Matt Stokes, Julie Raymond, and Angela Pacini. Thanks also to Anne Yourt, Robin Dwarka, Ashley Bristowe, and Conrad Schickedanz.

Thanks to my fellow writers: Jacqueline Valenica, Paul Vermeersch, Andrew F. Sullivan, Mat Laporte, Lisa de Nikolits, Terri Favro, Gary Barwin, Elan Mastai, Carolyn Black, and Sandra Kasturi.

Thanks to my family: Frances MacFarlane, Don MacFarlane, Don Pasquella, Dennis Boatright, Andrew

Pasquella, Margie Niedzwiecki, Randy Niedzwiecki, Jacob Niedzwiecki, Anand Mahadevan, Thaba Niedzwiecki, and Phet Sayo.

Extra big thanks to my wife, Emma Niedzwiecki, and to my kids, Leah and Matthew. I love you all so much.

Mystery and Crime Fiction from Dundurn Press

Birder Murder Mysteries
by Steve Burrows
(Birding, British Coastal Town Mysteries)
A Siege of Bitterns
A Pitying of Doves
A Cast of Falcons
A Shimmer of Hummingbirds
A Tiding of Magpies
A Dance of Cranes

Amanda Doucette Mysteries
by Barbara Fradkin
(Female Sleuth, Wilderness)
Fire in the Stars
The Trickster's Lullaby
Prisoners of Hope

B.C. Blues Crime
by R.M. Greenaway
(British Columbia, Police Procedural)
Cold Girl
Undertow
Creep
Flights and Falls
Coming soon: River of Lies

Victor Lessard Thrillers
by Martin Michaud
(Quebec Thriller, Police Procedural)
Never Forget

Stonechild & Rouleau Mysteries
by Brenda Chapman
(Indigenous Sleuth, Kingston, Police Procedural)
Cold Mourning
Butterfly Kills
Tumbled Graves
Shallow End
Bleeding Darkness
Turning Secrets
Coming soon: Closing Time

The Candace Starr Series
by C.S. O'Cinneide
(Noir, Hitwoman, Dark Humour)
The Starr Sting Scale

Tell Me My Name
by Erin Ruddy
(Domestic Thriller, Dark Secrets)

Jenny Willson Mysteries
by Dave Butler
(National Parks, Animal Protection)
Full Curl
No Place for Wolverines
In Rhino We Trust

Creature X Mysteries
by J.J. Dupuis
(Cryptozoology, Female Sleuth)
Coming soon: Roanoke Ridge

The Walking Shadows
by Brenden Carlson
(Alternate History, Robots)
Coming soon: Night Call

Jack Palace Series
by A.G. Pasquella
(Noir, Toronto, Mob)
Yard Dog
Carve the Heart

The Falls Mysteries
by J.E. Barnard
(Rural Alberta, Female Sleuth)
When the Flood Falls
Where the Ice Falls
Coming soon: Why the Rock Falls

Dan Sharp Mysteries
by Jeffrey Round
(LGBTQ, Toronto)
Lake on the Mountain
Pumpkin Eater
The Jade Butterfly
After the Horses

The God Game
Shadow Puppet
Lion's Head Revisited

True Patriots
by Russell Fralich
(POLITICAL THRILLER, MILITARY, ALT RIGHT)

Max O'Brien Mysteries
by Mario Bolduc
(POLITICAL THRILLER, CON MAN)
The Kashmir Trap
The Roma Plot
The Tanzania Conspiracy

Cullen and Cobb Mysteries
by David A. Poulsen
(CALGARY, PRIVATE INVESTIGATORS, ORGANIZED CRIME)
Serpents Rising
Dead Air
Last Song Sung
None So Deadly

Jack Taggart Mysteries
by Don Easton
(UNDERCOVER OPERATIONS)
Loose Ends
Above Ground
Angel in the Full Moon
Samurai Code
Dead Ends
Birds of a Feather
Corporate Asset
The Benefactor
Art and Murder
A Delicate Matter
Subverting Justice
An Element of Risk
The Grey Zone

Crang Mysteries
by Jack Batten
(HUMOUR, TORONTO)
Crang Plays the Ace
Straight No Chaser

Riviera Blues
Blood Count
Take Five
Keeper of the Flame
Booking In

Border City Blues
by Michael Januska
(PROHIBITION-ERA WINDSOR)
Maiden Lane
Riverside Drive
Prospect Avenue
Coming soon: *St. Luke Road*

Foreign Affairs Mysteries
by Nick Wilkshire
(GLOBAL CRIME FICTION, HUMOUR)
Escape to Havana
The Moscow Code
Remember Tokyo

Inspector Green Mysteries
by Barbara Fradkin
(OTTAWA, POLICE PROCEDURAL)
Do or Die
Once Upon a Time
Mist Walker
Fifth Son
Honour Among Men
Dream Chasers
This Thing of Darkness
Beautiful Lie the Dead
The Whisper of Legends
None So Blind

Lies That Bind
by Penelope Williams
(RURAL ONTARIO, AMATEUR SLEUTH)